"Sweetheart, Those Bedroom Eyes Of Yours Are Eloquent Liars."

"They aren't deceiving you," Blayne said. "I boarded that plane wanting you. That hasn't changed one iota. Given the opportunity, I still want to make love to you."

"Make love?" Sunny scoffed, ignoring the tenderness in his voice. "Make *lust*. A polite form of lying is saying one word and meaning another."

"Make love," he repeated firmly.

"You don't know the meaning of love any more than you know the meaning of deception. Love 'em and leave 'em. That's your motto. No thanks." The desire for revenge pumped through her veins, igniting her temper. "My idea of loving involves something more than a few nights together every seven years or so."

He gingerly leaned toward her, angry at her for maligning what they'd shared. "I'm not going to argue—"

"You always turned your back on me rather than fight fair," Sunny argued.

"You always got belligerent when you knew you were wrong."

"Prove I'm wrong."

Dear Reader,

Welcome to Silhouette! Our goal is to give you hours of unbeatable reading pleasure, and we hope you'll enjoy each month's six new Silhouette Desires. These sensual, provocative love stories are both believable and compelling—sometimes they're poignant, sometimes humorous, but always enjoyable.

Indulge yourself. Experience all the passion and excitement of falling in love along with our heroine as she meets the irresistible man of her dreams and together they overcome all obstacles in the path to a happy ending.

If this is your first Desire, I hope it'll be the first of many. If you're already a Silhouette Desire reader, thanks for your support! Look for some of your favorite authors in the coming months: Stephanie James, Diana Palmer, Dixie Browning, Ann Major and Doreen Owens Malek, to name just a few.

Happy reading!

Isabel Swift
Senior Editor

SDRL-7/85

JO ANN ALGERMISSEN
Made in America

Silhouette Desire

Published by Silhouette Books New York

America's Publisher of Contemporary Romance

SILHOUETTE BOOKS
300 East 42nd St., New York, N.Y. 10017

ISBN: 0-373-05361-4

First Silhouette Books printing July 1987

America's Publisher of Contemporary Romance

Printed in the U.S.A.

JO ANN ALGERMISSEN

believes in love, be it romantic love, sibling love, parental love or love of books. She's given and received them all. Ms. Algermissen and her husband of twenty years live on Kiawah Island in South Carolina with their two children, a weimaraner and three horses. She considers herself one lucky lady. Jo Ann also writes under the pseudonym Anna Hudson.

Dedicated to a "Grand Old Lady"
who recently received a face-lift
and the modern-day patriots that cared enough
to make it possible.

One

"Merry Christmas, Sunny!" the postman called, ignoring the midsummer heat and the multitude of red, white and blue flags flying over the door. He gave a hearty "ho-ho-ho!" waved and left the shop.

"Merry Christmas to you, too!" she returned, a bit puzzled by his off-season greeting. Costumed in a replica of Uncle Sam's red-and-white striped pants with a blue jacket and a stovepipe hat, she felt certain Al hadn't mistaken her for Santa Claus. Seasonal costumes worn by Sunny were part of the charm of the Holiday Shoppe.

She finished rolling a poster of the Statue of Liberty that had been the backdrop of her Fourth of July window display and hurried to the counter, where Al had deposited the mail.

Jean Ann, affectionately dubbed Sunny by her family and friends, checked the return addresses. She sorted the mail into two piles: business and personal. Blithely she ignored the bills, placing them in a neat stack for Starr, her sister and business partner, to pay.

Bright red and green envelopes explained Al's greeting. Distributors of hand-crafted Christmas items were preparing early for the holiday season. Postmarks from around the world widened the broad smile that was as much Sunny's business trademark as an expression of her optimistic outlook on life.

"For a woman who's been in North Carolina since she was twelve..." Her thoughts dwindled as she reached the bottom of the stack.

A telegram? Good news seldom came via a telegram. Could it be a delayed shipment? Dreading to open the envelope, she wondered what items would be most likely to be shipped late.

"Must be the Rudolphs," she deduced, since they were the featured item she'd preordered. The candy-wrapped, blinking-red-nosed reindeers had been a hit last season. They were in such demand that she'd had to reorder them twice. As a precaution against making the same mistake again, she'd placed her order way in advance.

She ripped open the telegram and read silently:

JEAN ANN PEIPER
c/o HOLIDAY SHOPPE
RALEIGH, NORTH CAROLINA
WILL BE IN RALEIGH JUNE 30 STOP WANT
TO SEE CHILD STOP WILL CALL UPON
ARRIVAL STOP

BLAYNE MACCAFFREY

Her hands visibly shaking, Sunny smoothed the sharp creases in the yellow paper across the glass countertop before she reread the message. On rubbery legs she crossed to the beanbag chair and collapsed into it.

Blayne MacCaffrey was coming back to Raleigh and wanted to see his child!

What child?

There was no child for him to see!

Sunny held her forehead. Her fingers massaged her temples as if that would help her to think more clearly. With crystal clarity she remembered the parting remark she'd made right before he climbed on the airplane seven years ago bound for the Middle East.

"I could be pregnant!" she'd shouted, tears streaming down her youthful face.

Desperate situations called for drastic measures, didn't they? She'd been extremely desperate. At twenty-one, she'd thought her world was ending.

Blayne had turned for a moment. The pained expression on his face told her it would have been kinder to shoot him in the back. His face took on a grim expression. "I'll take care of you."

He'd take care of her, she repeated silently, glancing once again at the telegram. Why couldn't Blayne have been like a million other irresponsible young men in a similar situation? Why hadn't he just deserted her completely? Much to her chagrin, he *had* taken care of her... financially.

Her world hadn't ended then; she hadn't been pregnant; she'd survived. Sunny blinked to clear her vision from a sudden spurt of tears. But what about now? Despite the fife and drum music coming from the record player in the back of the shop that promised victory with every drumroll, her immediate future looked precarious.

Handling money had always been a bone of contention between Blayne and herself. From the time they'd been kids growing up next door to each other, they'd always disagreed on its value.

Blayne saved money, saying he was preparing for a rainy day. Sunny spent money as freely as she smiled. Why worry about rainy days? The sun would always come out again. Money burned a hole in her pocket. One minute it was there and the next minute it disappeared. Could she help it if the weekly allowance she received from her grandfather only lasted from Sunday to Wednesday? There were simply too many sun-drenched days in a week.

On many occasions when she'd run out of money, she'd scampered next door to Blayne. "The old ant and the grasshopper story," Blayne would say disapprovingly. There wasn't a doubt in Sunny's mind that Blayne would still have the first dollar he'd earned as a grocery store bagger if she hadn't talked him into spending it on a record they'd both wanted. To Blayne, being financially responsible had been a sign of maturity.

Yes, she'd borrowed money from him, but she'd always paid him back . . . eventually. She rationalized that paying a debt demonstrated her maturity. She wasn't immature. Why didn't Blayne see her generosity as a positive personality trait rather than a flaw?

"The tightwad and the spendthrift," she murmured as she shifted her weight in the beanbag chair. She shook her head, knowing she was being unfair to Blayne. She definitely was a spendthrift, but Blayne wasn't a tightwad. He kept a close eye on his money, but he wasn't a penny-pincher.

She glanced at the cartoon drawing tacked on to the wall behind the cash register. Blayne had drawn it while he was in college, and given it to her as a gag gift. A comical dragon, butterball fat, rested against a tree picking his teeth with a rolled-up ten-dollar bill. Pieces of dollar bills with her name printed on them were strewed on the ground. Blayne had given her the cartoon to remind her to keep a close eye on her money.

"The money dragon wins again."

Sunny grimaced. Blayne's going to wish he'd kept a close eye on me when he discovers his child was merely wishful thinking, she thought. When he returns and finds himself childless, he'll have every right to do me in.

She'd done some crazy things in her life, but accepting the special delivery letter that contained his cashier's check had to qualify her as a certifiable loony.

Thinking back, she recalled how she'd reacted when the check arrived. The betrayal and hurt she'd felt when he'd left had changed to anger. Damn it, he'd left her high and dry to help untangle a corporate computer system in some godforsaken country she couldn't even find on a world map! He'd callously taken everything she had to give and cavalierly tossed it aside to chase the wind. Feeling self-righteous, she'd decided that he obviously didn't need the money or he wouldn't have sent it. Why not take it? Although her anger momentarily justified her attitude, she had quickly changed her mind.

Determined to show Blayne how mature she was, she'd contacted his employer to get his exact whereabouts. Company policy prohibited the secretary Sunny spoke to from giving out Blayne's address; however she promised to forward any letters Sunny wished to send. Without a second thought, Sunny put his check in an envelope with a brief note explaining that she was not pregnant. Feeling decidedly adult, she'd licked the stamp and mailed the letter.

A month later, the envelope, check and letter she'd written were returned unopened, inside a larger brown envelope. The secretary she'd spoken to included an impersonal cover letter explaining that Blayne was now working for another company with computer problems. Although the company that originally hired him had tried to forward her letter, it had eventually been returned.

After mulling over myriad ideas as to what to do with his check, she finally put it in a savings account for safekeeping. She'd intended to prove to Blayne she wasn't careless or immature. Rain or shine, she promised herself she'd save it and return it, if and when he came back to Raleigh.

As the years went on and she didn't hear from Blayne, she'd blocked the reason behind the savings account from her mind. It seemed like Blayne didn't care about her or the money, and it also seemed that he had no intention of ever returning to Raleigh. When an emergency arose, or a needy cause presented itself, she'd dip into her "Santa Claus fund." Once or twice she'd even giggled at the thought of Blayne fixing Santa Claus's computer at the North Pole to finance her benevolence. Surely he wouldn't mind spending his guilt money on worthy causes.

Searching her memory, she tried to recall exactly which worthwhile causes she had financed. Keeping track of money from one month to the next was difficult. Trying to pinpoint where the illusive green stuff went during a seven-year period was nearly impossible.

She felt certain she hadn't spent a dime of the money on herself. There always seemed to be someone she loved who was in a financial crisis, especially Starr. She knew she'd given her sister money two years ago to help pay Starr's divorce lawyer. Maybe she could get it back before Blayne arrived.

Sunny struggled out of the beanbag chair. The telegram slid to the polished floor. She rushed to the phone and dialed Starr's number. She could almost hear the money dragon on the wall chuckling over her predicament.

"Starr! I need some money. Fast!" she babbled, sounding more hysterical with each word.

"Haven't you heard the old saying that charity begins at home? Who are you donating money to this time?"

"It doesn't matter, does it?" Mentally she started to tabulate the extent of her debt. Damn those zeros. Where did the decimal point belong? Her eyes widened with alarm as she eliminated the decimal point all together. It couldn't be *that* much! "How much is twelve times seven times eighteen percent?"

"About one thousand five hundred. I can lend you a hundred or so, but—"

"Fifteen thousand!" Sunny wailed, adding the missing zeros. "It can't be! I couldn't have spent that much!" *Fifteen thousand* dollars! She gulped. She hadn't the vaguest notion of how much money was still in the savings account, but she was certain it was far less than her debt. "Oh, Starr! I'm in trouble. Big time."

"Sunny, calm down. You're always in trouble with money. You know I wouldn't say this if I didn't love you, but you'd have given the Holiday Shoppe away years ago if I hadn't been around to run the financial end of it." Starr sighed patiently. "Whatever arrived COD, just give Al a check. I'll cover it."

"Write a check!" She mouthed the amount, then gasped. She pivoted, giving the money dragon a dirty look. Was her imagination playing tricks on her, or had the smirk on the dragon's face widened? "Do we have enough for me to leave the country?"

"In the middle of the summer season? Our inventory is at an all-time high. Besides, you wouldn't leave the U.S. of A. unless..." She muffled the mouthpiece with her hand and shouted, "Russell! Randy! Quit bickering! Is that gum I see in your hand, Russell Mitchell? Don't you dare! I paid a small fortune for those braces! Randy, are you feeding the dog chocolate pudding from your own spoon! Kids! All I have to do is get on the phone and..."

Sunny straightened as though a bolt of lightning had struck her. "Wait a minute! I paid for those braces!" *With Blayne's money,* she silently added. What else had she paid for? Russell's emergency appendectomy. Allergy shots.

The mental list ended when Starr said, "You think you've got money problems? School tuition went up again this year. I'll barely recover from forking out that money when I'll have Christmas staring me in the face. Want a kid for Christmas? Take two!"

"That's it!" Sunny chewed on her lip. Blayne wouldn't be here long. A couple of days. A week at the most. He'd be off solving computer problems in Timbuktu and never be the wiser. "Randy's six. I'll take him."

"What? You may be their favorite aunt, but it's because you give them everything they want, from mechanical cars to chocolate. The dermatologist—"

"I paid for the dermatologist, too!" she squawked. "Starr, this is an emergency. You've got to help." Sunny heard her sister gasp. "I'll only need Randy for a day or two and we'll call it even."

"For fifteen thousand dollars?" Starr shouted the number as though it were obscene. "Nobody has that kind of money! What have you gotten yourself into? I've told you a million times that your loosey-goosey way with money was going to get you into trouble. What is it? Gambling? Extortion?"

"Nothing illegal." Or was taking money under false pretenses illegal? She could have been pregnant with Blayne's child. Granted, she had accepted the money under false pretenses, his not hers, so she couldn't legally be held liable. Could she? What difference did legalities make? Dead people don't serve time. Blayne MacCaffrey was a man of action. He wouldn't wait for the slow wheels of justice. He was a trouble-shooter; she was trouble. He had every right to shoot her.

"Jean Ann Peiper, you're up to something. You'd better tell me about it now!"

Sunny flinched at the parental tone Starr used. "Do you remember Blayne MacCaffrey?"

"Well, I'm not likely to forget the man you wept buckets of tears over when he went to Africa."

"The Middle East," Sunny corrected timidly.

"The moon! Who cares where he went? I had to put up with your sniffling and sniveling while I was combating morning sickness."

"He sent me some money." A lump lodged in Sunny's throat momentarily blocking her speech.

"What for?"

"To support his child," Sunny croaked.

"What child? You don't have a child!"

"Right," Sunny moaned. "That's the problem."

Starr paused. "Oh, my Lord. Now I get the picture. You told him you were pregnant to keep him here. He left but sent child support. You need money to pay him back because there isn't a Baby Mac-Caffrey. Am I right in assuming that we can expect a visit from Blayne shortly?"

Sunny nodded, too choked up to speak. Clearing her throat, she asked, "What am I gonna do?"

For long seconds neither of them spoke as they considered Sunny's options. Finally Starr said, "Blayne MacCaffrey sent you money to pay for his guilt. You shouldn't deny him that privilege."

"What?" Sunny whispered.

"You heard me. He's just like my dear ex-husband, Joe. Once a month he feels guilty about not seeing his sons and trots himself in here like some sort of white knight. He takes the kids somewhere fabulous that I can't afford. He assuages his guilt feelings by throwing money at the boys. He's the hero in their lives and I'm the Wicked Witch of the West because I'm here daily to discipline them."

"You lost me, Starr. What does Joe have to do with Blayne?"

"It's the same principle. If you did have a kid, Baby MacCaffrey would be dazzled by Blayne arriving with an armload of gifts. Blayne, like Joe, would be like Santa Claus to the kid." Her tone became sardonic. "And I can guarantee, when Blayne's guilt feelings subsided, he'd be out of here quicker than a blink of Santa's eye."

"That's irrelevant!" Sunny protested. "I don't have a kid! I've got to figure out a way to pay back the money!"

"And absolve him of his guilt? Let Blayne sue you if he's got the guts. He's exactly like my ex. Both of them think it's okay for a man to vanish when the children need him, but not a woman. Well," Starr snapped, "I've tweaked his nose a time or two!"

Sunny groaned in protest. Although she was certain her sister was still very fond of her ex-husband, Starr had never completely gotten over her divorce. A tiny smile tugged at the corner of Sunny's lips when she remembered the latest method Starr had used to tweak Joe's nose. When he'd been late with his child-support payment, Starr had signed him up for children's magazines; the subscription rate equaled the amount of the missing payment. No doubt, Joe couldn't walk by a magazine rack without thinking: did I put the payment in the mail?

Starr laughed as she too recalled her minor victory. "It's called creative revenge. Don't get mad, get even . . . cleverly. I'm here to tell you, it gave me great pleasure knowing my ex would be receiving fifty-five children's magazines for the next year. One way or another, he's going to pay the Peiper, pardon the pun.''

"But, Starr, you got even with Joe for *not* sending a payment. My problem is just the reverse. Blayne sent support for a child I don't have. He paid the Peiper...both Peipers. I used the vast majority of the money I spent to help you.''

"And that's why I'm going to sacrifice and help you,'' Starr replied thoughtfully.

"You are?'' Relief flooded through Sunny. "You've got some money stashed away?''

"Not a dime.''

The money dragon roared with glee.

Sunny's hope of instantly repaying Blayne faded. She should have known Starr wasn't able to pay back any of the loans. There had to be a way. She rubbed her chin thoughtfully. If only Blayne had decided to return in October, things would have been different. They could have used the consignment money for the Christmas trees that would be cut off her grandfather's farm to repay him.

Mentally Sunny pictured herself haughtily handing Blayne a check for the full amount and saying something like, "Here's your money. You didn't think I was mature enough to hang on to it, did you?''

Maturity was the main issue between herself and Blayne, not the cashier's check.

Her eyes widened as she thought of a brilliant solution. "I've got it! We'll give Blayne a postdated check for the Christmas trees we'll harvest in October off of Granddad's farm. We'll have to eat beans for months, but—"

"Not a dime!" While Sunny had been thinking, Starr had been conjuring up a few ideas of her own. "I mean it. Not one red cent."

"Starr! Blayne is going to kill me!"

"Don't be overly dramatic. You're going to give him exactly what he deserves."

"I am?"

"A good swift kick where it would do the most damage is too good for him. We'll really hit him where it hurts!"

"I'm not going to like this," Sunny muttered, certain Starr was thinking up a bit of creative revenge against Blayne. Sunny stifled the urge to slam the phone down before Starr started to convince her to do something she knew would only get her deeper into trouble. "Whatever you're thinking, never mind, Starr. You'll come up with something like you did when I failed math. Remember? You talked me into putting a firecracker in the math teacher's mailbox."

"Yeah, but I also remember the triumphant look on your face when you heard it go boom!"

Sunny sighed. "All I remember is being scared silly by the postal authorities. Whatever you're hatching, forget it."

"Why, Sunny," Starr said, chuckling, "it was your idea to borrow Randy. You can borrow him with my blessings."

Why did Sunny's brilliant idea sound so devious when she heard it repeated by her sister? It had been an impulsive, half-baked idea when she'd thought of it, but now, knowing how her sister's mind worked, she expected Starr to present a master plan that would be a major strike on behalf of the sisterhood of women in general, and Sunny in particular.

"It wouldn't work," Sunny stated emphatically. "Do you think there's enough credit left on the MasterCard account to get me to Brazil?"

"You aren't going to run, Jean Ann Peiper. If you did by some major miracle manage to climb aboard a plane bound for a foreign country, you'd parachute out right before you crossed the U.S. border. Stick around. Face the music. You're going to like the sound of it more than you think."

"Know any funeral dirges?" Sunny quipped. "Blayne arrives tomorrow."

"Where's your optimistic outlook on life?"

"Inside the money dragon's belly."

"You're an easy touch. Toughen up. Blayne dumped you. Get mad! Better yet, get even. Blayne MacCaffrey broke your heart by using you like a doormat to wipe his feet on. Think of how your life would have been changed if you had been pregnant."

Sunny put her hand over her ear, which was totally ineffective. Starr had always been able to make the illogical sound logical. "A postdated check nailed to the door, with me out of firing range, sounds smarter."

"No, little sister. Half of the money from the sale of those trees is mine."

"What? Are you telling me I can't have the tree money? Starr, I spent most of Blayne's money on you and the kids. I'm calling in all your loans!" The second she'd spoken, Sunny knew how empty her words were. She couldn't dun anybody for money. She got red-faced and flustered collecting for Easter Seals.

"I'm offering to do something better than repay the loans. I'm offering to rent Randy to you for the weekend. You said Mr. Fly-by-night Knight won't be around here longer than that."

Sunny straightened. She wasn't going to let Starr bully her into doing something she was certain would get her deeper into trouble. When the Peiper sisters were volatile teenagers and were arguing, one word could end the dispute: *compromise.*

"Compromise," Sunny shouted before Starr could convince her to do something outrageous.

"Okay, okay," Starr agreed, recognizing the steely tone of her sister's voice. "We'll compromise. What are the terms?"

"Like it or not, we pay the money back. That's only fair."

Starr groaned, "You and your damned sense of fair play. Did MacCaffrey play fair when he left you?"

"No, he didn't. But he isn't going to like his part of the compromise, either. He eventually gets his money, but Blayne won't get out of this scot-free. I wasn't pregnant, but I could have been. Money doesn't absolve him of his paternal responsibility. I'll borrow Randy. Randy is a superspecial six-year-old child. Having Randy around will show Blayne exactly what he could have been missing all these years. When Blayne gets ready to board the plane, I'll tell him who Randy is and give him a postdated check.''

''Sounds fair until you hit the 'give him a check' part. Is that negotiable?''

''Absolutely not. In fact, you'll have to figure out how much compounded interest I owe him.'' Calculating interest was beyond Sunny's mathematical ability.

''No interest payment. If I had my way, you'd—''

''Compromise,'' Sunny finished decisively.

''All right. You win, I'll figure out the interest payment.'' Starr agreed grudgingly. ''I'll tell Randy he's going to pretend to be your son. He'll love it. Personality-wise, he's more like you than me, anyway.''

Sunny chuckled. ''He's a handful. Send him over early in the morning and he can help put the mechanical toys together for the shop.''

''You're really asking for trouble. The kid's some sort of weirdo genius when it comes to anything mechanical. Yesterday I caught him trying to disassemble the lawnmower. I won't buy him a go-cart, so he decided he'd build one. Sound familiar?''

''Are you referring to *our* attempt to convert our bikes into motorcycles?''

Starr giggled girlishly. ''We were pretty outrageous back then, weren't we?''

''Yeah. The only kids worse were Preacher Hagan's twins. Chad was the worst of the two. Nobody back then would have believed that he would grow up to be a florist. He was the terror of the neighborhood.''

Both women readily laughed at the shared memory.

''Speaking of Chad,'' Sunny said with a matchmaking twinkle in her eyes, ''he just placed an early order for ten candy Christmas wreaths. Three peppermint. Four assorted candies. Two strawberry.''

''That's nine, Sunny,'' Starr corrected, exasperation evident in her voice. ''You have a real mental block about numbers.''

Sunny covered the smirk on her face as though her sister could see through the telephone wires. Simple addition was easy for her, especially if money wasn't involved. She knew exactly how many wreaths she had sold. Adopting what she hoped was her best businesslike voice, she suggested, ''Guess you'd better go see him about the order. Take a twig of mistletoe with you. Bye.''

She hung up before Starr could argue. For months Sunny had suspected Chad was trying to work up his courage to ask Starr for a date. A tiny little nudge in the right direction might result in Starr's finding the happiness she richly deserved.

Chad Hagan, despite his teenage pranks, was the kind of guy that would be around twenty years from now. Quite unlike Blayne MacCaffrey, she thought.

As she flipped through Christmas cards from around the world, she realized she'd lived in more countries than the typical American visited during a lifetime. Her father had been a career officer in the military forces. With what seemed like capriciousness on the part of the army, he'd been transferred from pillar to post and taken his family with him.

As a teenager, Blayne had been intrigued by her travels while she'd envied his growing up in a stable environment. He had roots. Blayne scoffed at the word. He believed people with roots ran the risk of becoming stagnant. Foreign cities and countries lured him away from his roots. But, to Sunny, far away places with unpronounceable names all had one thing in common: they were inhabited by strangers.

Automatically Sunny blocked from her mind the penalties of being a stranger in a hostile country. The two American flags that had been presented to her grandfather at her parents' funeral were stored in the attic, along with other painful childhood memories. Digging up the past wasn't necessary. She'd learned the hard way the value of having roots, and friends, and a place to call home.

"Home's a place to put your Christmas tree," she said, turning toward the front display window, mentally removing the Fourth of July decorations and replacing them with shimmering Christmas trees. She'd compensated for the years in her childhood when having a gaily decorated tree had been impossible. The trees she decorated were eventually sold, but that was irrelevant. They brought joy and happiness into the lives of others. That's what mattered to Sunny.

She raised her chin stubbornly. Much as she disliked Starr's idea of creative revenge, she realized she must protect herself in some way from what Blayne would consider current proof of her lack of maturity. But why was that so important to her? she wondered. She hadn't seen Blayne in seven years, and during that time she'd tried to forget that she'd once loved him. Yet the prospect of his return was strangely disturbing, disturbing in a way that wasn't entirely due to the money she owed him.

She glanced around the shop trying to visualize the contents through Blayne's eyes. Confident everything was neat and tidy, and yet appealingly displayed, she nodded her head with firm resolution. Years ago he'd hurt her deeply by telling her to grow up and face the world, Sunny remembered, lost in thought. "I'll show him I've grown up...without him," she murmured.

The telephone jangled.

"Holiday Shoppe," Sunny answered.

"It's me, again," Starr said. "I've thought of a little extra dose of creative revenge for Blayne. You know that shirt in the display window?"

"The one with the Statue of Liberty on the front?"

"No, no, no. The maternity shirt that has 'Made In The U.S.A.' stenciled on the front. Why don't you stuff a pillow down your front—"

Sunny banged the phone into its cradle and shook her head.

"Revenge can only go so far," she muttered. Tomorrow when Blayne arrived, she wasn't going to look like an inflated balloon. She was going to look cool and sophisticated...grown up.

Two

Blayne MacCaffrey watched his reflection mirrored in the display windows as he crossed the parklike area where the Holiday Shoppe was located. Satisfied his limp was barely discernible, he wiped his brow with the back of his hand. Unless he wanted to validate Sunny's almost pathological fear of travel to foreign countries, he'd have to make certain she couldn't detect the damage a bomb fragment had caused.

An amused smile stretched over his angular features. Beneath a carved wooden sign, a sculptured replica of Paul Revere astride a horse stood on the sidewalk in front of the store. "Holiday Shoppe," Blayne read aloud, his voice abnormally husky.

Sunny had always been partial to the Fourth of July, he remembered. Paul Revere represented her idea of a bold, stouthearted hero; Betsy Ross symbolized courage and determination. He smiled again as he recalled Sunny dressing up as a female patriot for Halloween and bribing the younger children to choose patriot costumes by giving them an extra handful of chocolate treats.

Once he'd teased her, asking if she had "Made in America" tattooed on the soles of her feet.

His heart hammered in his chest as long-forgotten memories surfaced. He cupped his hand beside his eyes to block the sunshine and peered through the plate-glass window, searching for a glimpse of Sunny.

What he saw made his chin drop.

Sunny, dressed in some sort of frilly colonial costume, was crouched on all fours sorting through a box of toys with a young boy. Absorbed in what she was doing, she hadn't noticed that her long dress had bunched behind her knees. White lace edging her pantaloons accented her slender calves and dainty ankles. A stranger could almost have mistaken her for the boy's playmate.

Blayne didn't. He immediately recognized the slender sensuous hips as belonging to Sunny. Hundreds of times while they were growing up he'd seen her similarly occupied. Sunny had a knack of devoting all her attention in one direction and totally ignoring what was taking place in the rest of the world.

He watched her hand a toy soldier to the redheaded child. He clenched his teeth; his lips thinned into a straight line.

Who was the boy?

Whoever the child was, Blayne knew for certain that he wasn't his father.

Within months of leaving Raleigh, he'd become part of the Americans Abroad Network that sent him the Raleigh newspaper and kept him attuned to local news. Later on, a computer technician who graduated from the University of North Carolina in Chapel Hill relayed information regarding Sunny. Although he'd been out of the States, he knew of any major events in her life, including her opening the Holiday Shoppe.

"What's she up to?" Blayne muttered, intrigued. His callused hand raked through his hair. "More important, after being so damned clever with your telegram, how the hell are you going to tell her you know that kid isn't yours?"

Because of the unexpected turn of events and the raw emotions they brought about, Blayne decided to watch for a few minutes. Perhaps he'd glean a few clues as to what was going on.

Unaware of the man at the window, Sunny sat back on her heels and ruffled Randy's hair. "You can take the soldiers outside, but don't lose them."

"I'll be supercareful, Aunt Sunny."

"Mom," Sunny corrected.

"Oh, yeah. Mom. I keep forgetting about Mom's rent-a-kid-for-a-day idea." He grinned, then self-consciously covered his mouth to hide the gaping space where two front teeth were missing. His eyebrows drew together thoughtfully. "You aren't gonna get married, are you?"

She chuckled, watching her nephew stuff a soldier in each pocket of his shirt and shorts. "Someday. Maybe."

"That's not what Mom says."

"Oh, yeah? Exactly what did dear old *Aunt* Starr have to say?"

"First she explained about playing a little joke on the guy that used to live next door to you, but then she said something about you turning into a flustrated..." Randy paused, knowing he'd used the wrong word. "Fluttered?"

"Frustrated?"

"Yeah! Some of Mom's big words are hard to remember 'cause her sentences don't make sense."

Squinting, Randy examined the uniform of the soldier in his hand as if he had told Sunny all she needed to know.

"Frustrated," she prompted.

"Frustrated old made." He looked from the toy soldier to Sunny's face. Her strange smile was something like the one his mother had once made when he'd told her he'd eaten a worm. "I said it didn't make sense. How can *made* be frustrated? See? I told you I couldn't remember the big words when the little words don't make sense."

"*Made* and *maid* sound alike, but they're two different words. An unmarried girl used to be called a maiden. I guess somewhere back in history the word was shortened to maid.''

''I couldn't figure out what she meant from the rest of the stuff Mom said.'' Randy shook his head. ''That didn't make much sense, either. Sometimes Mom can be real spacey.''

''Oh?''

''She said you want a kid, but couldn't have one until you got married. Everybody knows you don't have to get married to have a kid.'' Randy's cheeks turned bright pink, accenting the crop of freckles across the bridge of his pug nose. ''I mean...well, you know. Mom isn't married, but she has Russell and me.''

''But, Randy, your mother was married when she had both of you,'' Sunny replied. ''Your dad doesn't live with you...''

Randy giggled, rising to his feet. As if confiding a great secret, he whispered, ''He's gonna move back home.''

''Hmm,'' she replied noncommittally. Certain Randy had misunderstood something he'd overheard, she raised to her knees and asked, ''What makes you think your dad is coming home?''

''Mom says Dad will get smart sooner or later. And Dad says it's worse being divorced to Mom than being married to her. That doesn't make much sense.'' He smiled wistfully. ''But I figure since they both say they love Russell and me, that Dad'll come home soon—maybe by Christmas.''

Hugging Randy, Sunny kissed him on the top of his head. She didn't have the heart to tell him that there wasn't much hope his parents would get back together.

"That's all I want for Christmas," Randy told her. His thin arms wrapped around Sunny's neck, squeezing it hard.

A huge lump swelled in Sunny's throat, leaving her speechless. She knew she should say something wise, something that would prepare Randy for his upcoming disappointment, but words failed her.

Suddenly the sleigh bells over the door jangled, intruding on their conversation, and Randy and Sunny turned toward the sound. Bright sunshine haloed the man standing in the door. His features were shadowed, but a delicious tingle centering in her chest told Sunny that Blayne MacCaffrey had arrived.

He seemed taller, broader than she remembered. Gone was the boyish roundness of his cheeks. His face was lean and hard. Sunlight played in his golden hair, and her pulse began to flutter.

How could she have forgotten that Blayne was so handsome? Realizing the physical attraction she had felt so many years ago was undiminished, she wished he'd come back fat and bald. He'd broken her heart once, and with a sinking feeling, Sunny realized he probably had the power to do it again.

Caught between Randy's hopes for the future and this vision from the past, Sunny struggled for composure. Unaware of her own movement, she gracefully rose. All the clever, witty greetings she'd prepared were forgotten.

Randy glanced from the tall stranger with the stern look on his face to his aunt's bewildered expression. Protectively, he wrapped one arm around Sunny's waist and laced his fingers through hers. Her hands were cold and limp.

Letting the door swing shut, Blayne entered the shop. The anger that had been slowly building as he'd watched Sunny and the child through the window faded into nothingness. His mouth felt dry.

He'd intended to storm into the shop and demand to know whose child Sunny was holding in her arms. He'd seen the fleeting kiss and the loving hug she'd given the little boy. But that wasn't his son she was bestowing motherly affection upon. Whose kid was it?

She stared at him, and for an instant there was no look of recognition in her blue eyes. My God, she doesn't even remember me, he mused silently, his male ego thoroughly deflated.

Sunny swallowed to relieve the uncomfortably tight feeling in her throat. With a great deal of effort she managed to say, "Welcome home, Blayne."

Her eyes sparkled with moisture. He'd changed, and yet, he was the same. She'd expected him to be tanned from traveling around the world, but his face was pale, almost chalky white. Thin lines were etched on his forehead. She looked down at the floor, as if embarrassed to have stared so intently at him.

The strong body was heartbreakingly familiar. How many times had her fingers caressed that body, lovingly entwined themselves in the golden hair on his chest?

"Thanks," Blayne muttered. His jaw ached from having clenched his teeth. His heart ached, too.

"I'm Randy." Stepping between the two adults, the little boy awkwardly extended his hand. Sensing the stranger was the man his aunt had been waiting for, he glanced over his shoulder and winked at Sunny before adding, "My mom and my aunt own this store."

Randy's formal introduction jarred Sunny's malfunctioning mind back into action. She'd promised Starr to stick to the compromise they'd agreed to, but now, face-to-face with Blayne, the decision clawed at her heart. The half smile Blayne gave Randy reminded her of the indulgent smiles he'd given her as he'd handed her money to help her stretch her allowance from Wednesday through to Sunday.

Blayne restrained himself from demanding, "Who's your father?" as he accepted the child's small hand. In a stilted voice, he replied mechanically, "Nice to meet you, Randy."

"Can I go outside and play with the soldiers now?" Randy asked, pivoting on one foot to face his aunt. Exasperated, he looked toward the ceiling as if to say, "What's with you? Cat got your tongue?"

"Sure." Sunny forced a weak smile.

"See ya," Randy whooped, then streaked through the door.

Blayne watched Sunny's expression. There had been a time when he could read her face like an open book. Her bright eyes followed the child with unmistakable affection. Could his information possibly have been wrong? The bonds of love flowing between Sunny and the boy who claimed to be her son were obvious. He couldn't deny that Randy must belong to her.

"He seems like a well-mannered kid," Blayne commented. "You've done a good job of raising him alone."

"I've had help." Determined to avoid lying to Blayne unless absolutely necessary, she glanced toward the window to elude his penetrating eyes. Slowly she moved in the same direction until her back was to him. She couldn't tell the whole truth, but she'd decided to stick as close to it as possible. "Starr spends a lot of time with him."

A dark curl peeking from beneath the lacy headdress at her nape threatened to undo Blayne's taut control. His fingers were reaching toward it before he realized what he was doing. For most of his life, she'd enchanted him. Blayne balled his fingers and shoved them into his pocket.

An awkward silence hung between them. Finally curiosity got the best of Sunny. She quickly glanced over her shoulder. His pensive expression sent a shiver down her spine. Blayne hadn't won a full scholarship to Duke University by being the class idiot. Bit by bit he was unraveling the clues he'd been given to solve the mystery.

Hoping to throw him off the track, she said, "Randy is a lot like you."

"How?"

His bad knee almost buckled as he stepped closer. The doctor had warned him not to put stress on the injured joint by standing for very long except when necessary. Grateful she hadn't seen the jerky movement, he debated whether or not to collapse into the beanbag chair near the display cabinet. Sinking into it would be simple; getting up would be impossible. He wasn't about to literally crawl around on the floor to get back on his feet in front of Sunny.

Sunny surreptitiously watched his face beneath her lowered lashes. The thought of Randy being his child seemed to pain him. Guilt pierced her heart. Revenge was supposed to be sweet. Why was she feeling like a Benedict Arnold? He was the one who had betrayed her by leaving, not the other way around. True, he had pleaded with her to go with him, but he'd known how living in a foreign country was impossible for her. He'd left her when she could have been pregnant, she reminded herself. Their child could have been the little boy outside playing with tin soldiers.

"How?" Blayne repeated. Her remote coolness contrasted sharply with the nickname he'd given her. Although they were scant inches apart, she was holding back, giving him the cold shoulder. Each lie she told, he thought, would serve as an icy block with which he would build an impenetrable wall between them. Later, when his defenses were fortified and he was safe, he'd tell her that he'd heard she wasn't pregnant when he'd left Raleigh.

His warm breath whispered across the loose curls on her neck, making them quiver deliciously against her sensitive skin. He hadn't so much as touched her, but his nearness made her heart pound rapidly. She took a deep breath to steady her nerves as she tucked some wayward curls under the elastic band. Her wits scattered when she removed her hand, leaving her nape vulnerable.

"He's good with his hands," she blurted.

Blayne chuckled with delight at the blush coloring Sunny's cheeks. She wasn't impervious to him. The memory of how she'd responded to his caresses thawed the icy barrier he'd been mentally erecting between them.

She shot him a look that clearly cursed him for making her blush the same way she had as a teenager when he'd teased her unmercifully. He must have told her a million and one times to think before she opened her mouth.

"What I meant is that he loves his computer games more than any other toy."

Deciding Blayne was too close for comfort, she turned from the window. She'd planned on marching indignantly away from him, but he was too quick. He easily captured her wrist before she could escape.

"Does he have a bratty little girl next door who gets her jollies beating him at his own games?" he asked teasingly.

"Russell has that pleasure."

"Who's Russell?"

"His b... big buddy, Starr's son. You remember him; he was just a baby when you left." He'd almost caught her off balance with his question. Side-stepping the truth while attempting to keep her emotions under a tight rein was difficult. "They play together."

"While you're running the shop?"

His thumb tormented the delicate skin under her pulse point. She was mesmerized by the small circular motion, unable to look away. "Yes. I run the shop while Starr takes care of the kids and does the bookkeeping," she murmured.

"Convenient. Doesn't what's-his-name, Starr's husband, object? I seem to recall his wanting Starr to get a job outside the house."

"Joe," she said quietly. "They're divorced."

His thumb trekked across the fleshy mound beneath her thumb onto the sensitive skin of her palm. Reflexively her fingers curled around his thumb, warm and responsive. He wondered what would happen if he boldly pulled her against him. Would her arms twine around his shoulder as easily as her fingers had wound around his thumb? Should he be brave enough to kiss her, would she respond? His eyes blazed, fueled by his thoughts.

"I'm sorry," he responded sympathetically. "I know how much Starr loved him." *As much as you said you loved me.*

"Love comes and goes for the Peiper sisters." She jerked her hand from his and looked up, straight into Blayne's eyes. "We don't seem to be able to hold on to our men."

"Sweetheart, you knew I had to leave Raleigh."

Sunny couldn't deny his claim. She had known from the beginning. For years he'd asked her over and over to tell him what she remembered about the foreign cities in which she'd lived. His bedroom walls had been plastered with travel posters and brochures. She couldn't deny being aware of his desire to see the four corners of the earth.

The past was irreversible. But what about the here and now?

She was light years away from being the naive, immature woman she'd been when he'd left. She wanted to know the worst. Sunny braced her shoulders, preparing for a verbal slap. "And you'll leave again, won't you?" she demanded.

He watched her take a deep breath. A lie would be kinder than the truth, he thought, but replied yes.

"Damn your honesty." She stepped backward until the wooden railing surrounding the elevated window display barred further retreat.

Damn your deception. Blayne cornered her by gripping the rail beside her shoulders. His hands blocked her attempt to escape. "Would you rather have me lie to you?"

Yes, she wanted to shout. Make sweet promises of eternal love. Make me believe them. She choked back the plea she'd made years ago: *Please don't leave me!*

For a single moment she came close to hating Blayne MacCaffrey. With one word he'd destroyed the hopes and dreams she'd subconsciously cherished. Her hands twisted her apron into knots.

"Deception isn't restricted to big, bold lies," she said, her hurt adding barbs to each word.

"Meaning?"

"Unspoken lies." In the last fifteen minutes she'd become an expert at letting Blayne make assumptions while she remained silent. But she wasn't the only one in the shop who specialized in half-truths. Her blue eyes flashed angrily at him. "While you were holding my hand, were you thinking about fixing computer foul-ups in Timbuktu?"

She saw him shake his head slowly.

Scornfully she said, "Sweetheart, those bedroom eyes of yours are eloquent liars." His blue eyes promised forever, but meant only today.

"They aren't deceiving you," he said, sounding sincere. "I boarded that plane wanting you. That hasn't changed one iota. Given the opportunity, I still want to make love with you."

"Make love?" she scoffed, ignoring the tenderness in his voice. "Make *lust*. A polite form of lying is saying one word and meaning another."

"Make love," he repeated firmly. His knee twinged painfully, reminding him of the real reason he'd told Sunny that he had to leave her again.

"You don't know the meaning of love any more than you know the meaning of deception. Love 'em and leave 'em. That's your motto. No thanks." The desire for revenge pumped through her veins, igniting her temper. "My idea of loving involves something more than a few nights together every seven years or so."

He gingerly leaned toward her, sorely tempted to shake her for maligning what they'd shared. "I'm not going to argue..."

"Of course not! Silence is another form of deception." She banged the flat of her hand on the glass like a judge pounding a gavel. Guilty! He'd sentenced himself to prolonging her silence regarding Randy's parentage. "You always turned your back on me rather than fight fair."

"And you always got belligerent when you knew you were wrong."

"Prove I'm wrong."

"How?"

She pointed toward the park in front of the shop where Randy played with the tin soldiers. "Define father."

Starr passed in front of her finger outside the plate-glass window. Reinforcements, Sunny thought, thankful for the arrival of her sister. Her defenses had weakened when he'd mentioned making love to her. Much as she denied wanting him, being this close activated her vivid imagination.

Although Blayne's temper was slow to rouse, Sunny had exposed a raw nerve. Angered, he was determined to explode the myth between them right here and now. Randy wasn't his child. "With pleasure," he snarled. "A child's biological father is the man who—"

"Hi!" Starr greeted over the sound of the sleigh bells noisily interrupting Blayne. She eyed him up and down, lifted her nose and said to her sister, "I've come to get your boy. Remember? You promised to let Randy spend the weekend at my house.''

"Don't you think the boy should spend some time with his father?" Blayne asked, deciding he didn't want anyone else present when he confronted Sunny with the truth. A thin veneer of congeniality hid his inner turmoil.

"Why bother?" Starr responded icily. "A child doesn't miss something he hasn't had. Don't you have a plane to catch or something?"

Blayne shrugged, refusing to commit himself one way or another. He watched as the sisters passed silent signals. Starr had a smug, triumphant smile; Sunny looked as though she were slowly coming apart at the seams.

He'd forgotten how Starr had managed to drag Sunny into one scrape after another throughout their teenage years. Back then, as now, he was the one who had to stop them before things got out of hand. He turned his head to keep them from seeing the grin tugging at the corner of his lips. The Peiper sisters had forgotten something, too.

He loved solving mysteries. His ability to solve intricate problems was what had made him successful as a troubleshooter in the computer industry. Experience had taught him that the solution to problems was always readily available. If he reworked the program, paying close attention to small details, eventually the glitch could be found.

Ladies, prepare to have your program analyzed for glitches!

"Starr is right," Blayne agreed. "I've neglected Randy. I owe it to him to stick around for a while."

"No!" Sunny cried.

"How long?" Starr demanded, her smugness changing to wariness.

"A week. A month." His eyes moved from Starr to Sunny. "However long it takes to discover the meaning of the word *father*." He coughed to keep from chuckling. Their mouths were hanging open. He could almost hear the gears in their minds grinding to a halt. "No time like the present to begin," he added. "If you'll excuse me, I'll go outside and start getting acquainted with my son."

The door had barely swung closed when Sunny grabbed Starr's arm. "Look what you've done!"

"Me? You must have said something to make him stick around. What'd you do? Tell him he was a lousy father?"

"Not exactly," Sunny said, hedging. "I told you this was a harebrained idea. Creative revenge! Humph!"

"It's working, isn't it?"

"No!"

"Yes, sister dear, it is. Didn't you get a teensy-weensy thrill when you introduced him to Randy?"

"No."

Sunny couldn't tell Starr that the only thrill she'd gotten was when Blayne was within touching distance. Lord, how did she get herself into these messes? She'd promised herself to remain aloof. Aloof? She'd practically swooned the moment she'd seen him.

"Come on, Sunny. Stop looking as though Christmas has been called off for lack of interest," Starr jeered, moving toward the front window. "You're doing great! Blayne..."

"Isn't going to leave. Didn't you hear him?"

"You can handle him. Who knows? You've done such a good job of snowing him that he may give you another check!"

"That's not funny. Besides, I'm worried. We can't leave him alone with Randy too long. The kid's only six years old; he is bound to make some slipup and spill the beans. And if Blayne stays in town more than a day or two, he might run into old friends who could tell him that I don't have a child." She stuck her hands in front of her. "Look at my hands. I'm shaking like a leaf in a wind storm."

"Put 'em in your apron pocket."

"You and your simple solutions can go straight to—"

"Tsk, tsk, tsk. Time to get out Granddad's bar of soap?"

Sunny made a fist with one hand and shook it in her sister's direction. "You don't know Blayne as well as I do. He's no dummy. I haven't had to lie to him yet, but the minute I do he's going to see right through me."

Chuckling over Sunny being clever enough to pass Randy off as Blayne's son without lying, Starr crossed to Sunny's side and gave her a big hug. "It's working. Don't worry about Randy. We coached him really well, and that kid has enough of his mother in him to come through with flying colors in a situation like this. As far as Blayne's meeting old friends goes, you're crazy if you think he's going to rush to look up people he's been out of contact with for seven years. Think of it this way...if Blayne sticks around until we harvest the Christmas trees, you might be able to pay him off in full."

Starr's reassurance fell flat. "The trees aren't harvested until October. By then I'll be what's cut down and hauled away."

"Cheer up. Once the grass starts growing under Blayne's feet, they'll start to itch and he'll leave."

Sunny hid her face in her hands to keep Starr from seeing her reaction to the thought of Blayne leaving. Unwanted tears gathered in her eyes.

The sleigh bells ringing drew them apart. Sunny turned her back to Starr and used the corner of her apron to wipe her eyes.

"Something caught in your eye?" Al, the postman asked, lifting her chin with the stack of mail in his hand.

Relieved that it wasn't Blayne who'd seen her cloud up, Sunny nodded. "I got it."

Al grinned. "Isn't that Blayne MacCaffrey outside playing soldiers with Randy?"

"Did you say anything to him?" Starr asked, alert to the possibility of Al's having ruined the whole set-up.

"No. I wasn't sure it was him. It's been a long time since he's been in these parts. Guess that's because his parents passed away. Hey, you girls used to be his neighbors, didn't you? Sure, I remember now. You two used to be thick as thieves. Starr was always getting you into mischief, and Blayne was always getting you out of it. My, my, it sure makes me realize how old I'm getting.''

"You're not getting old," Sunny protested kindly.

"Retirement's only a year away." He looked around the shop. "Got anything new and special I can get as a gift for my mother's birthday?"

"Nothing she doesn't have," Sunny replied, knowing Al's mother's birthday was on the Fourth of July. "The last time I was at her house, I took her one of the T-shirts in the window because it's her favorite slogan."

Al smiled. "The 'Made in The U.S.A.' shirt? I'm having a tough time getting it off of her to wash it."

Starr rolled her eyes to the ceiling in dismay, then glanced at the money dragon cartoon. Sunny gave away more than she sold. Here was a customer, who was practically begging to put money in the cash register, and Sunny tells him there isn't one item in the shop for sale. No wonder they had money problems.

"What about the paperweights that just arrived?" Starr prompted. "The ones with the Statue of Liberty on the inside. Turn it upside down and little silver stars flutter around like snowflakes."

"Thanks for reminding me." Sunny walked behind the glass counter and pulled out a gaily wrapped package. She handed it to Al as she took the mail. "With company from out of town, I may not have time to drop by your mother's."

"You're always giving her little treasures. Are you sure I can't pay you for this?" Al offered, reaching into his pocket.

"If you insist." Starr shot Sunny a dirty look. "We could use the money."

"No," Sunny said. "We don't need the money that badly."

"You're hopeless," Starr said and groaned. "Before long we're going to be reduced to eating beans and—"

"Hush up, Starr." Her voice shook. Fond as she was of Al and his mother, Sunny knew how they loved to talk about the people Al saw on his rounds. Telephone, telegraph and tell Al. "Give Opal a hug for me," she added, hoping to erase the worried frown on the postman's face.

"I don't mind paying. You've always been good to Mom." He took another look around the shop. "What about a poster?"

"You plan on decorating the ceiling?" Sunny teased. "Her walls are papered with them."

"You must have something I can buy. I'd hate to see your store go out of business."

Starr had the good grace to flush with embarrassment. "I'd better get Randy," she said.

"Let him take the soldiers with him. I said he could." Sunny walked to the door with Starr and Al.

Al paused at the doorway. "I almost forgot to tell you about the fireworks display being canceled."

"Canceled? Why?" Starr asked.

"Insurance. City Hall says the premium has sky-rocketed. Opal sure is going to be disappointed. She thinks the fireworks are the highlight of her birthday party. A few of the downtown businesses are kicking in to hire an attorney. I don't suppose the Holiday Shoppe could afford to—"

"Fourth of July without fireworks? Of course, we'll help." Sunny ignored Starr's look of dismay. Nodding in the direction where Blayne and Randy were playing with the soldiers, she threatened in a soft voice, "Write him a check or you're going to see some real fireworks around here."

Shrugging, Starr pulled the checkbook from her purse, found out who to make the check out to and began filling in the blanks. "Maybe the same lawyer will represent us when we file for bankruptcy," she muttered as she wrote.

"Generosity is a virtue," Sunny whispered with conviction.

"Sure it is," Starr grumbled. "And as long as we're spouting platitudes, don't forget the one about money being the root of all evil." She ripped the check from the checkbook, kissed it and handed it to Al. "You'd also do well to remember the one about the road to hell being paved with good intentions."

Al laughed. "You don't have to worry about Sunny. She's already considered an angel by everybody in town, always there when she's needed."

"Hmm," Starr replied skeptically. "Too bad the banker won't accept angels' wings and halos as collateral on a loan."

Shifting uncomfortably from foot to foot, Al watched the silent fireworks exploding between the two sisters. "I'm running late. Thanks."

"I hope you're going to be happy living in the poorhouse," Starr muttered, signaling Randy to pack up and get ready to go home.

"Stop worrying about the poorhouse. See the grin on Blayne's face? Something tells me that means we're in trouble . . . big trouble."

Three

___

Blayne heaved himself to his feet, trying to ignore a twinge of pain. "Promise?"

"Cross my heart and hope to die," Randy swore solemnly making an *X* on his chest. "It's our secret. Mom would ground me forever if I told her."

Lightly draping his arm across Randy's shoulders, Blayne said, "You didn't tell me anything I didn't already know. If I had a son, I'd want him to be just like you."

"Oh yeah?" His small chest expanded with pride. "You're not so bad yourself. For an old man, you play soldiers real good."

Tossing his head back, Blayne laughed. Five minutes with Randy had erased any doubts he had regarding the overseas network giving him the wrong information. Starr's son had the same slap-caress way of speaking his mother used.

Randy's comment reminded him of an incident he'd forgotten. Now he could almost hear Starr the first time he'd picked Sunny up for a real date. "You look nice in your white shirt, but what's that smell?" she'd asked innocently.

A self-conscious adolescent, he'd suffered the entire evening, not knowing if he'd splashed too much after-shave on his cheeks or had forgotten to use deodorant. For months he'd avoided being around Sunny's big sister. When Starr confronted him, calling him stuck-up, she'd been sincerely amazed to learn her careless remark had offended him. She'd actually thought she was being kind.

Does Starr think she's being kind by letting Sunny borrow Randy? His speculation ceased when Randy tugged on his shirt front.

"Can we play soldiers tomorrow?"

"Tomorrow?"

"Uh-huh. Aunt Sunny eats dinner at our house on Sunday. We don't have to play soldiers. I've got a neat video game Aunt Sunny gave me. Froggie. Ever played Froggie?"

Laughing wickedly, Blayne replied, "Randy, I'm a champion at playing Froggie."

"Really?"

"I've certainly kept your aunt hopping, haven't I?"

Randy giggled, glancing toward the front of the store where his mother and aunt stood watching them.

Sunny frowned, turning toward her sister. "Did you hear Blayne laugh?"

"Yeah, and I'm not sure I like the sound of it."

"Shh," Sunny warned nervously, "he's close enough to hear us."

"Hey, Mom!" Randy ran toward Starr, then at the last moment veered into Sunny's legs. "Do I still get to take the soldiers along with me?"

"You bet, tiger." Sunny dropped to her knees. "Give me a hug and a kiss."

"Big boys don't kiss," he protested, squirming from her arms, darting down the sidewalk toward the parking lot. "C'mon, M . . . A-Aunt Starr. I'm gonna miss the late-afternoon soldier program on television."

"Talk to you later," Starr said as she rushed to keep up with Randy. "Be careful!"

Sunny wasn't certain whether her sister was calling to Randy or to herself. Her face turned beet red when Blayne helped her to her feet and murmured near her ear, "Shall we name the next one after her?"

"There won't be a *next* one."

His eyes twinkled mischievously, totally oblivious to her retort.

"You don't want Randy to be an only child, do you?" he teased. "I'm in favor of six or seven."

Feeling as though her face were on fire, she asked, "How much is seven times seven, plus twenty-eight?"

"Seventy-seven."

"Don't you think seventy-seven is a bit old for a pregnant lady? You're only in town once every seven years!"

Blayne pretended to give the subject serious thought. "How much is twenty-eight plus six times nine months?"

She hadn't the vaguest idea what the answer would be, but she clearly understood what he meant: for the next six years, she'd have his child every nine months. Hope flared, dying quickly. He'd told her he wasn't planning on returning to Raleigh. Unless...oh, no, she thought. Randy must have really turned on the charm. Blayne was considering staying for Randy's sake, and while he was tied down with one child he might as well beget more.

Their eyes met, unwavering, intense. His were blue as the summer sky. They beckoned her into their depths. Her heart skipped a beat. Recollections she'd locked in the far recesses of her mind burst into her consciousness. She felt as though he'd climbed inside her skin to force her to unlock her memories of him.

"Don't do this to me, Blayne," she whispered in a choked voice, unable to break the invisible hold he had on her soul. "I died a little when you boarded the plane. Go. Go now, please."

"I won't leave until you go with me."

"I can't."

"You can." His fingers curled around her upper arms. Ignoring the curious stares of the people passing on the nearby sidewalk, he turned her toward the mirrored reflection of the shop window. "Look at yourself. You aren't Betsy Ross, and it's not the eighteenth century. Look hard. What do you see?"

His hand removed her cap, and her hair, dark and full, fell to her shoulders. His thumb and forefinger stroked her nape.

"Flags. Red. White. Blue. Stars. America...law and order...safety...roots...*Christmas trees*."

"They're in your mind. You can take them anywhere."

"You can; I can't. Don't pull me apart again. Go."

"Look closely at what's in the window. How many of those items have Japan, West Germany or England stamped on the bottom?"

Her pale eyes lingered on a carved eagle, symbol of America's strength. She pointed to it. "A man in the Rocky Mountains of Colorado carved it. When I opened the shipping box, I could smell pine needles. See the log cabin. Tennessee. It can be taken apart and rebuilt. Inside it is a tiny replica of a potbellied stove, a braided rug, handmade maple furniture. Look there." Her hand moved toward an ebony horse, rearing on its hind legs. "Georgia clay and a Kentucky craftsman."

She looked at Blayne. "I don't have to go anywhere to appreciate what's here. But I have. Last fall I went to Michigan. Where are the lakes bluer or the apple orchards more fragrant? The year before, I went to Florida. Sand dollars...seashells as big as both of my hands. I've seen the giant Sequoia in California. Did you know the rain in Oregon is misty? It feels like sunshine on your skin. Blayne, I don't have to go anywhere. Everything is all here in the good old U.S. of A.''

From the slow shake of his head, she knew she hadn't convinced him. She had to keep trying to make him understand.

"Our country is beautiful, but what impressed me most was the people. In Wisconsin I could close my eyes, listen to the Swedish accent and pretend I was in the Scandinavian countries. In Florida there are shops where only Spanish is spoken, and there's a Chinatown in San Francisco. I thought of you and asked myself, why would these people leave their homes, their loved ones, their heritage? Why did they uproot themselves and come here? Famine and political upheaval are great motivators, but...why did they stay? Maybe they feel the way I do when I'm at Granddad's farm or walking by the modern buildings downtown. America is so...'' She paused, searching for the right word. "New. Yeah, that's the word. Just a little over two hundred years *new*. And yet we have the wisdom of thousands of years given as a special gift by the immigrants who came here seeking freedom.''

She pointed toward the Statue of Liberty poster. "A gift from France. I guess that makes her an immigrant, too. I remember flying into New York, after—'' her throat clogged ''—bringing Mom and Dad to Arlington Cemetery. I was a kid. Scared. Hurt. But I'll never forget how I felt when I saw the Statue of Liberty. Raleigh is a long way from her, but I felt as though I was coming home.''

"And you promised yourself you'd never leave," Blayne said, recalling the first time he'd seen her. His heart had gone out to her. He'd also been young, but he'd made a promise, too. Whatever the cost, he'd protect and love her.

Promises made by the young are the hardest to keep, he thought.

He doubted if anyone had caused Sunny more pain than he had. She'd begged him to stay; he'd gone. Now she begged him to go, but he knew he'd stay. Sunny Peiper was a vital part of him, a part he should have acknowledged years ago.

With an ironic twist of fate, her fear of leaving home had become his. The mere thought of entering an airport in a foreign country made him break out in a cold sweat. Flashbacks haunted him.

Everything had happened too fast. One minute he'd been whistling as he collected his luggage from the conveyor belt, and the next minute the world around him had exploded. In his worst nightmares, he could still feel the world spin, hear the shouts and screams, see himself brutally thrown by the impact of the explosion. Then the sterile whiteness of bedsheets covering his elevated leg was his next memory.

He could have died.

During his lengthy hospitalization he had restructured his goals in life based on that realization. Seven years of traveling in twenty-six countries had taken its toll on his long streak of good luck. For years he'd taken numerous risks believing himself indestructible, but recently he'd discarded the naive idea that his

American passport would shield him against danger. When he was in a hostile environment he was as vulnerable as any other foreigner. His intention of going everywhere and seeing everything waned, and like a wounded animal, he wanted to go home.

Home and Sunny were synonymous. Apprehensive as to how she would receive his return, he'd guaranteed himself a foot in the door by sending the telegram. They'd pulled hundreds of pranks on each other. He felt confident Sunny would read it, laugh and open her arms to welcome him home.

Thoughts of Sunny had kept him from going crazy when he left the hospital on his way to the airport. His stomach had twisted in knots of fear. Only a mental picture of Sunny had kept his feet moving forward through the narrow tunnel leading to the plane.

"I'll never leave," Sunny reiterated. Drawn by the agony clouding his eyes, she leaned backward against him. "Do you understand why?"

Blayne nodded. No matter how much Sunny said it was her love for the U.S. that kept her from leaving, Blayne knew that was only partially true. Fear had kept her from traveling with him, and now it had brought them back together. He couldn't let fear dominate their happiness. Together they could conquer anything.

She turned too late to see his grim determination. "We were best friends long before we were lovers," she said softly. "I missed you, but you've always been with me. In my travels I used to catch myself—"

"Pointing something out to me?" Blayne smiled tenderly and brushed her bangs off her forehead.

He'd tried the "you woman, me man" approach and failed. Patience wasn't his strong point. He preferred to make a quick decision, then follow through full speed ahead, but Sunny wasn't going to be stampeded into renewing their relationship. He'd have to take it slow and try to build from their long friendship.

"How did you know?"

"Because I caught myself doing the same thing. I was on a camel in the middle of the Sahara Desert, and I found myself wanting to make certain you noticed how the sand shifted until it looked like giant blond waves. Another time, when I was skiing down a slope in Switzerland, I glanced over my shoulder expecting to see you zipping along behind me."

Sunny grinned. "I'm a terrible skier. You left me on the baby slopes and skied with your fraternity brothers, remember?"

She loved the way laugh lines creased the corners of his eyes. His chuckle rumbled in his chest.

"I was protecting you." His finger skied down her pert nose, lingering on the corner of her lips.

"From your friends?"

"From the pine trees. Every time you saw one you hugged it. Your cheeks had a bark burn."

"Bark burn!" she hooted. "Don't you mean whisker burn? You were growing your first beard."

"First and last. You threatened to shave it off with the lawnmower while I was sleeping."

Sunny shook her head. "I'd forgotten the wild threats I used to make."

"Hmm." He leaned down and reminded her of the threat she'd made if she so much as saw him looking at another woman. Her instantaneous blush made him smile. "Very possessive, weren't you?"

"How can you say that? You were always on my case about giving away everything I owned."

"You did. Your closet was perpetually empty because you loaned your clothes to your girlfriends. Your bike was always in front of someone else's house. What about your first car?"

She punched him playfully, refusing to admit a girlfriend of hers had wrecked it before she'd put fifty miles on the odometer.

"I'll bet you still can't go into a store without dropping coins into those plastic containers collecting for various charities. We'd get to the checkout counter and you'd be penniless. I'd have to buy you a pack of gum or a candy bar."

"I didn't ask you to buy me anything. And I always paid you back."

"Ha! I'd be a rich man if you paid me everything you owed me."

Too close to the truth, Sunny thought. Turning on her heel, she marched toward the shop door.

"Hey, where are you going?"

"Inside. I have to go fight the money dragon."

"Come on, Sunny." He tried to grab her elbow, but she was too fast. His bum knee wasn't cooperating. "I was teasing you. What do you think I'm going to do?

Repossess your shop for old debts? Haven't you heard about the seven-year statute of limitations?''

The door slammed in his face. He grabbed for the doorknob, futilely twisting it. ''Sunny, you can't make money if you...'' A sign in the middle of the door was flipped from Welcome to Closed—Come Back Later. He pounded on the glass. ''Unlock the door! I know you can hear me. Let me in!''

''Not by the hair on my chinny-chin-chin,'' a small voice said behind him. ''Are you supposed to be the big, bad wolf?''

A pint-sized girl in scruffy jeans and torn T-shirt eyed Blayne warily.

He raked his hand through his hair. ''No.''

''Miz Sunny don't like you?''

The understatement of the year, Blayne thought, saying, ''She's . . . busy.''

''I gotta give her somethin'.'' Her pigtails dipped to her waist as she raised on tiptoe and tried to see into the shop. ''I can't wait. My mom don't like for me to be gone too long.''

''I'll be here until the shop reopens. Can I give it to her?''

Brown eyes scrutinized him from head to toe. She shoved her hand into her jeans pocket. ''You don't look down-and-out,'' she muttered, obviously not certain she was a good judge of character.

His knee throbbed; he couldn't stoop down and re-assure her. He smiled, hoping his friendliness would build confidence.

She pulled her hand from her pocket and slowly opened her tightly clenched fist. "This is all I got, mister. Two dimes and three pennies. Will you give it to Miz Sunny?"

"What's it for?"

"Just give it to her. Tell her it's from Cindy," the little girl said after a slight hesitation.

She dropped the coins into his hand and ran down the sidewalk, pigtails bouncing before Blayne could say anything.

"Tell her I love her," Blayne heard as the child rounded the corner.

Out of the mouths of babes, he mused. Those were the exact sentiments he wanted to express.

Sunny barely cracked the door open. "Did I hear Cindy's voice?" she asked, frowning slightly.

"Yes. She left some money for you."

"Money?" The crack widened. "What for?"

"She ran off before I could find out anything." He dropped the dimes and pennies into her hand. They were still warm from the child's body heat. "She said to tell you that she loves you."

"I don't understand," Sunny said, her argument with Blayne momentarily forgotten. "Where did Cindy get twenty-three cents?"

"From her parents, I imagine."

"Not likely. Her father lost his job, and her mother can't work because she has to take care of Cindy's brothers and sisters. You love a good mystery. Figure this one out."

"She'll probably be back to solve the mystery."

"But something else happened that's odd. I found a wrinkled five-dollar bill by the cash register. I didn't see anyone come in the shop while we were talking, did you?"

"No. Could someone have come in the back door? Is it locked?"

Jingling the coins in her hand, Sunny strode to the rear of the shop. She tested the handle on the door. It swung open. "Why would someone sneak in the back door and leave money here?"

"Lock the door. Next time you might not be so lucky."

"Don't you think this is strange?"

"Maybe the money fell out of Starr's purse while she was here. Or you could have been making change and forgotten to put it back in the register. Money doesn't appear out of nowhere. I'm certain there's a logical explanation for the twenty-three cents and the five-dollar bill. Put it in the cash register and quit worrying about it."

Sunny gave him a supercilious look. "Co-mingle funds? It takes me forever to balance the cash register without dropping in money that's unaccounted for. I'll put it in here, then I won't have to worry about it." She dropped it into a collection box labeled "Millbrook High School Band Uniform Fund."

"I don't want you to worry about money. That's why..."

"You sent me a cashier's check?" Sunny said, her heart beginning to pound.

"Partially."

Sunny pulled a tall stool from behind the counter for him before returning to the opposite side of the counter. She lifted a cardboard box filled with peppermint candy and florist wire and placed it between them.

"What's the other part?" she asked.

He watched her wrap a thin wire around one of the cellophane-wrapped candies. Her entire attention appeared focused on tying the candy in place. He smiled. Sunny always kept her hands busy when volatile subjects were being discussed.

"Guilt. I should have carried you aboard that plane instead of leaving you behind."

"A box of tissue would have sufficed," Sunny quipped. "Sending money wasn't necessary."

"Haven't you forgotten something? What about Randy?"

"He didn't need tissues."

"You're determined to be obtuse, aren't you?" He unwrapped a mint and popped it into his mouth.

Sunny grinned. "Tell me, Blayne, did you expect me to wait for you forever while you trotted around the globe?"

"No. I emphatically told you not to wait for me. That's why I didn't correspond. Letters would have built up your hopes."

"It would serve you right if I'd been happily married with five kids," Sunny muttered.

Blayne shifted the candy from one side of his mouth to the other. "Why didn't you marry?"

"Men are in short supply for a woman with a young child." Facts aren't lies, Sunny thought, justifying the way she was leading him to believe no one wanted her because of his child. "Would you marry a woman with another man's child?"

"The question never arose. I didn't form any lasting relationships while I was working abroad."

"Ahh, you were being true to your childhood sweetheart, right?" Her tone of voice clearly indicated she found that story hard to swallow. She wasn't going to let him believe she was the same naive, gullible woman he'd left behind.

"In my fashion," Blayne replied evasively.

"Oh, dear," Sunny mocked, "does that mean you're sending cashier's checks to the four corners of the earth?"

The peppermint went down the wrong way. Blayne strangled a cough; his face turned red. With great pleasure Sunny hopped down from her stool, skirted the counter and heartily pounded him on the back.

"Enough," Blayne said, raising his hands. He spun around on the stool, catching Sunny between his thighs. "You've had your revenge."

"I was only trying to help." She tried to break his grip. The more she squirmed, the tighter he held her with his powerful thighs. His hands moved to her waist and pulled her close.

"I'm willing to let you help me. Marry me."

Four

—————

Marry you?" Knocked off balance by his proposal and his tight hold on her, she toppled against his massive chest. She felt herself sinking deeper and deeper into his embrace. With difficulty she managed to ask, "Why?"

He cradled her closer and, despite herself, Sunny felt that this was where she belonged. Finally, he was home, and she was safe in his arms.

"Because I've thought of nothing for the last couple of months other than holding you."

"Why?" she repeated, her head spinning. He held her tighter as she fought to regain her equilibrium. She'd tried to resist the appeal she'd seen in his eyes. She'd thrown up roadblocks and detours when they'd traveled down Memory Lane, but it hadn't worked. After all these years she still loved him as much as she had the day he'd left her. For self-preservation, she had to stop his lips from driving her wild. He couldn't make love and talk at the same time, she reasoned. "Why?" she asked again.

"I love you," he answered simply.

"But I've changed; you've changed. We're—" her neck arched to give him easy access to the vulnerable places only he could make tingle "—strangers."

"Does this feel strange?" he asked, nibbling her earlobe, drawing a sensuous line with his tongue to the hollow below her neck. His fingers unbuttoned her collar. "Who knows you better?"

"No one," she conceded.

Her admission filled him with desire. No one. For seven long years she'd been faithful to his memory.

Feeling as if she were struggling for survival, she mimicked him, "I've been true...in my fashion."

"Liar," he accused gently. "You're mine. You've always been mine. I was just too stupid to know what I wanted. I want you, Sunny. Yesterday. Today. Tomorrow."

"No tomorrows," she whispered, her arms stealing around his neck. "Only today. Right now."

"We aren't kids, Sunny. We both want permanence."

"Have you changed your mind about leaving?" she whispered between kisses.

Although he wanted her desperately, he couldn't lie to her. "No."

Sunny suddenly became immobile in his arms. His fingers massaged the back of her waist. There was no mistaking his desire, but he touched her as though she were priceless crystal. And she felt every bit as fragile.

In her memory, his lovemaking had lacked such tenderness. He'd been passionate, wild, impatient years ago, never so gentle and sweet. She wanted to explore this new feeling, cherish it for as long as it lasted.

Her arms tightened. All the old need to be generous, to give herself to him surfaced. "Blayne, love me today. I won't ask for tomorrows. No tears. No regrets. I promise."

"Sweetheart," he groaned, rocking them together. Primitive urges surged through him, telling him to take her, to reclaim what was his. Her hand sliding from his thigh to his knee gave him the respite he needed. Pain from the wound temporarily obscured his driving need. "Sweetheart, we've got to wait until—"

"No. Isn't seven years long enough to wait?"

Despite his desire, he wanted the half-truths between them brought out into the open. Besides, he couldn't picture the two of them caught in the throes of passion should a customer decide to enter the shop. "Sunny, isn't there something you need to tell me?"

Sunny answered him by closing her lips over his. This wasn't the time for words; this was the time for action. Her tongue teased through the barrier of his teeth until it circled his. She heard his groan, felt him shudder, tasted the residue of mint.

She tingled with anticipation as his hand left her waist to slide between the ruffled bib apron and the calico fabric of her dress. His palm lazily circled against the tip of her breast before his fingers closed around it. A hot achiness settled between her legs.

Eyes closed, Sunny gave herself up to his sensuous kiss and touch. She wanted to be his more than she had ever wanted anything in her life. Sleigh bells jingled merrily, but she didn't hear them. She dismissed the hint of a hot summer's breeze and the sound of the front door being quietly closed. Nothing mattered, nothing but Blayne.

"Sunny?" a deep voice called from the door. "Uh, Sunny?"

A red tide of embarrassment crept up Blayne's face. He disengaged her arms from around his neck but kept her positioned between his thighs. The policeman standing in the doorway reminded him of another officer of the law, one he had seen standing beside his car many years before, flashing a light into the dark interior.

"We've got company," he said when Sunny's eyes fluttered open, dismay clearly readable in her expression.

Face flaming, she twisted toward the intruder. Blayne allowed her to turn but not to step toward the policeman. "Oh, uh—hi, Tim. Come in."

"Sorry to barge in. Would it be better if I came back later?" Tim asked, reluctant to add to Sunny's discomfort. He sized Blayne up with one quick look. "I thought I'd drop these off before I went on duty."

"Tim's wife makes pottery jack-o'-lanterns I sell at Halloween," Sunny explained to Blayne. Directing her question to Tim, she asked, "Is Jeanine getting an early start this year?"

"Nope. She's busy with the garden until late August. Bumper crop this year. She's canning more vegetables and fruit than we can use. Jeanine hates to waste anything." The mason jars in the sack he was carrying bumped together as he approached the counter. "We thought maybe you could use them."

"They'd be great for the Labor Day display. Did she put a price tag on each jar?"

"Jeanine doesn't want you to sell them. These are for you."

Sunny smiled at Tim as she watched him empty the sack, jar by jar, naming the contents. "Thanks. I haven't had home-canned food in years. I love it! Oh, I'm sorry, Tim. You haven't met Blayne MacCaffrey, have you?"

The two men shook hands, but the polite gesture soon developed into a knuckle-grinding contest on Tim's part. Momentarily caught unaware, Blayne winced, then increased the pressure of his grip.

"How long do you plan on visiting in Raleigh?" Tim asked casually as he lowered his hand to his side.

"I haven't made definite plans."

"Here on business or..."

Laughing, Sunny said, "Tim, you're cross-examining Blayne as though he were a vagrant. I'll personally vouch for his respectability."

"Sorry, Mr. MacCaffrey." His apology lacked conviction. "I guess I get a bit carried away with my duties. Raleigh's a great little city. Can't have strangers causing problems." The meaningful look he cast Blayne could have been fired from a six-shooter. "Right?"

"Right," Blayne agreed, uncertain of what Tim meant. Defensively he added, "I'm a law-abiding citizen at home for a short vacation."

The vaguely hostile looks passing between the two men dismayed Sunny. "Hey, what's going on, Tim? Does Blayne have a delinquent parking ticket or something?"

"An attractive, single woman can't be too careful," Tim answered, eyeing Blayne suspiciously. He retreated toward the door with a final warning. "You never can tell who you can really trust. I'll be keeping a close eye... on the shop."

Blayne understood the message perfectly. Tim would be keeping him under surveillance. "See you around," he said coolly.

"Thank Jeanine for me. I really appreciate getting the canned goods."

"No thanks are necessary. That's what friends are for, to help each other out." Tim tipped his hat and stalked out the door.

"What was that all about?" Blayne asked, crossing to the door.

Shrugging, Sunny joined him beside the front window. She glanced at the school clock hanging above the door, then flipped the lock. "I guess they appreciated my marketing Jeanine's pottery. It gives them extra money to spend on their kids for Christmas.''

"I wasn't referring to the food." Blayne watched Tim jog to the street where a patrol car waited. "Five will get you ten, he's running a check on me through headquarters.''

"Blayne, don't be ridiculous. Tim's doing his job. You're acting as paranoid as a thief getting ready to steal the crown jewels.''

"Anyone who's been under police observation in a foreign country instinctively knows when he's being watched. See how he keeps glancing toward the shop?''

Stepping up behind him, she wrapped her arms around his waist. "You're in America, not behind the Iron Curtain. Besides, Tim is my friend.''

Blayne shook off his apprehensiveness. "You're right. What's he going to find if he does check on me?''

"Nothing." She snuck a finger between the buttons of his shirt. "Well, almost nothing. You don't think the officer who patrols the back roads around Raleigh filed a report when he caught us, do you?''

His stomach quivered as she lightly trailed the tip of her finger across his taut flesh. "You thought of that incident, too? Both of us were scared witless.''

"Hmm." Her lips vibrated against his back as she chuckled. "You revved up the engine, shifted into first—''

"And plowed into the ditch. It took an hour for the tow truck to get the car back on the gravel road.''

"Which made it after midnight when I got home."

"I'll never forget your grandfather waiting for us on the front porch. I thought we were home free until he took the pipe from his mouth and said, 'All the hellin' in the world goes on after midnight, son.' He'd be glad to know I'm here to make an honorable woman of you," Blayne said teasingly.

Sunny pinched his backside. "Turn-of-the-century psychology," she said blithely, although she felt more guilty than ever. *Tell him Randy isn't his son,* her conscience prodded. *And don't forget to mention how you squandered his money. If you do, he'll think you're still an irresponsible kid.* She couldn't bring herself to tell him yet. She decided to throw him off track by stating another well-known fact. "Newspapers are filled with human interest stories about famous unmarried women who are raising children alone."

Wheeling around, Blayne gazed at her intensely. Wide-eyed, she worried her bottom lip between her teeth, then made a weak attempt to an innocent smile. Suddenly Blayne realized Sunny had never directly lied to him. She'd either nimbly avoided his questions or had made passing remarks about other women.

Whatever her motivation for refusing to level with him, it had to be powerful. What was she hiding behind her innocent smile? Blayne had met his share of deceitful people; unless love had totally blinded him, he felt certain Sunny wasn't one of them.

He considered confronting her. Certain she was incapable of telling an out-and-out lie, he said, "But most of the women you've read about would marry the father of their child, if given the opportunity.''

"I guess that's one of the differences between being famous and being *in*famous,'' she joked. Flippantly she added, "Kinda like the difference between being eccentric and being crazy. Money makes the difference.''

She's done it again, given an indirect, meaningless answer. Well, Sunny, he thought, I've played your game long enough. It's time for the rules to change.

Assuming a guilty look, he mumbled, "I'm sure it's difficult for you to forgive me for not being here while you were pregnant and for dropping out of sight for years. I don't blame you for refusing to accept my proposal. You're entitled to revenge. I was a rotten son-of-a...''

She clamped her hand over his mouth. "Hush. I won't allow you to say bad things about yourself. You did what you thought you had to do.''

Blayne almost wanted to drop to his knees and beg her forgiveness. He wanted to force her into absolving him of the crime he never really committed. But he couldn't do that. His infirmity would force him to be completely honest when she had to help him struggle to his feet. No, he must be careful not to overplay his hand.

"We've shared the good memories; now let's share the bad ones. How did you manage, unmarried and pregnant?''

"I don't want to...''

"*Please.*''

His earnest plea threw Sunny into a quandary. She could describe her sister's difficult pregnancy with detailed accuracy, but in doing so she'd be flagrantly lying. Backed into a corner, she attempted to wriggle free by using Starr's favorite phrase. "Randy made everything worth it."

Relentless in his pursuit of the truth, Blayne asked, "How much weight did you gain?"

"Doctors discourage excessive weight gain."

He pulled her arms in front of her until her fingertips touched. "This much?"

"Pregnant women are put on restricted diets," she mumbled, finding it more and more difficult to avoid answering his questions.

His hand covered her stomach. "Stretch marks?"

"Blayne!" she chastised, slapping his hand. "That's a terrible question."

"Between strangers, yes, but not between a woman and the father of her child. Is that why you haven't become involved with other men?"

"Now you're being ridiculous. A *real* man doesn't worry about stretch marks, or cellulite, or droopy bosoms." She folded her arms across her front when his gaze moved downward from her face. She caught the devilish twinkle in his eyes before he could conceal it. The faker!

Bosoms? What a quaint term. Blayne bit his tongue to keep from laughing aloud. Her pretense of righteous indignation tickled his sense of humor.

"Did your . . . bosom get larger?" he asked, careful to use the same word that she had used.

Preoccupied with dodging his questions, she'd forgotten how easily he had always been able to make her laugh. She'd forgotten how they'd teased and tormented each other throughout junior high and high school. They'd been the best of friends and sometimes the worst of enemies long before they'd become lovers.

She tried to look stern as she replied, "My bosoms grew larger and larger." Her hands indicating the enormous size to which they'd grown. "They went from apple size, to grapefruits, to cantaloupes, until they were huge as watermelons."

Blayne lost restraint first. Deep belly laughs shook him as his hands clamped around her waist, raising her high, spinning her around. Her melodic laughter joined his. For long minutes they stood, touching from shoulder to toe, laughing, enjoying each other's outrageous sense of the ridiculous.

"You should have seen the look on your face when I was describing how they grew."

"What about the prim way you said b-o-s-o-m-s," he asked, spelling the word. "You haven't given me a straight answer since I arrived."

"You asked the wrong questions," she blurted almost before she knew what she'd said.

He lowered her dangling feet to the floor. "Okay, sweetheart, try this question on for size. Who is Randy's father?"

Five

___

Sunny stared at him as if in shock. Her mind worked furiously, trying to find a way to answer Blayne's question without revealing the truth. But there was no way. He had her this time.

"I know Randy isn't our child, sweetheart. I've known for years." Without forethought he added, "I guess you owe me one, huh?"

"Confound it! You can't have known! The letter I sent was returned unopened." She spun from his arms, assimilating the latest bombshell he'd dropped. "How did you find out?" she demanded.

"Networking. It's easy for Americans abroad to find out what's going on at home." Blayne said. "No matter what you think, Sunny, I'd never have left you alone to fend for yourself if you really needed me."

He'd known all along, she realized. He'd been playing cat and mouse with her, waiting for her to make a mistake. "You can wipe the cat-who-caught-the-mouse look off your face. That was a rotten trick."

"Which one? My telegram or your passing Randy off as my long lost son? I'd say the score is even."

"I had good reasons for what I did," she fumed. "What about you?"

Blayne leaned on his good leg, crossing the other at the ankles. "Me, too. I'm willing to come to an amicable agreement."

"Humph! I heard what you said about owing you a kid. I don't give rain checks on making babies." She wanted to scream, *I don't owe you anything*. But her mouth had gotten her into enough trouble for one day. She did owe him. She owed him thousands of dollars. More than she could repay. "Your suggestion is hardly amicable when you're going to be leaving Raleigh soon."

"Come with me," Blayne coaxed. "Women have babies outside of the U.S.A. every day."

She poked his chest with her forefinger. "You know I've made up my mind. I'm not going anywhere. I love North Carolina."

"Let me see." He raised fingers as he began to list her loves. "You also love your sister and nephews." The plural of "nephew" hissed through his teeth unmistakably. "And you love your friends, acquaintances, cops, scruffy little girls, apple pie, hot dogs, home-canned food..." He took a deep breath. "I always wondered if you really loved *me*."

The wistful note in his voice cut through the defenses she'd begun to marshal. "Of course I loved you. Are you trying to be ridiculous, again? I told you I loved you every other breath."

"True, but when it came to choosing, you let me leave. You stayed with your other loves."

His logic eluded her. She'd stayed, but not because of her family and friends or other loves. She couldn't leave. Was her reason too simple for his analytical mind to comprehend?

"Logic! It was Starr's logic that convinced me to present Randy as your child. Randy is a son. Blayne wants a son. Therefore, Randy is Blayne's son. See where logic gets you? You don't need me to have a son. Why don't you find a rootless, logical woman?"

"Because I don't want any 'rootless, logical woman.' I want you." Before she could respond he said, "I'll take you to dinner, and we'll discuss the details. Get your purse."

"I can't go dressed like Betsy Ross. It's Saturday night. By the time I go home and change, the restaurants will be jam-packed."

"No excuses, Sunny. Remove the apron," he commanded, refusing to take no for an answer.

His fingers deftly opened the top three buttons of her dress. Although tempted to explore the expanse of soft skin, he hesitated. She'd responded to his touch earlier. Perhaps action, throwing her over his shoulder caveman-style, was the solution. No, he wanted more than a willing woman for an evening. He wanted commitment; a woman who loved him enough to follow him wherever he may have to go. His hands dropped to his sides.

"You've grown into a lovely woman, sweetheart. We'll go someplace special to celebrate my homecoming. Any recommendations?"

Aware that he was not giving her a choice as to whether or not to go to dinner with him, Sunny considered balking. Attraction fought with wariness. She wanted to be with him, and yet she knew she was asking for trouble. The less time she spent with him, the fewer tears she'd shed when he departed on a new assignment.

A smart, tough cookie like Starr would have tossed Blayne out the door and locked it behind him. What the heck, she thought finally, pulling on the bow that held her apron in place. She was a soft cookie; there was no denying it. She couldn't refuse.

"I'll call the Peachtree and make reservations," she said as she went to the counter to get her purse. The elegant restaurant would show Blayne that he didn't have to leave Raleigh to find something new and different. In seven years Raleigh had grown by leaps and bounds.

She dialed the number, watching Blayne remove a set of keys from his pocket. Good, she mused, he can drive. He wouldn't see the rattletrap she called her car. "Keith? Sunny Peiper. Any chance for reservations at this late date?"

Blayne felt a stab of possessiveness when he heard the warmth in her voice as she spoke on the phone to another man. Keith, who? he wondered, searching his mind for anyone named Keith.

"We'll have to hurry. They're booked solid after six." She locked the back door.

"Do I know Keith?" Blayne asked, assuming a nonchalant air. "Is he a local?"

Sunny grinned, knowing that for Blayne, a local was someone whose great-great-grandparents were from the immediate surrounding area. Their hometown had been close-knit until the past few years when thousands of people from all over the United States had moved to Raleigh.

"Remember Sonya? Keith's her husband. While they were in Atlanta, they met, married and returned here to open a restaurant." Her smile widened. "They'd be successful in any cosmopolitan city, but—"

"They returned to her hometown," Blayne said dryly. "Was that a subtle hint?"

"Raleigh has grown a lot and become a high-tech center. You could do your computer troubleshooting right here, but you won't."

"We'll see," Blayne replied, hesitant to indulge her dream of having him give up his footloose way of life.

Optimistic to the core, Sunny caught the glimmer of hope his answer held. "You're thinking about staying...permanently?"

Lie to me, her soulful eyes begged. Make me believe your lies.

Blayne considered sweet-talking her, telling her half-truths. His libido prodded him to do anything, say anything that would get her back to his suite at the Marriott. She wanted to believe him. With the slightest encouragement she'd follow him anywhere he wanted to take her—within the city limits of Raleigh.

Unfair tactic, Blayne chastised himself silently. In his idealistic youth, he'd been painfully honest with Sunny. He'd told her not to count on his return, and refused to let her cherish hopes of his eventual return through correspondence. Leaving Sunny behind was one of the toughest things he'd ever done. But he'd been man enough to face reality then. He couldn't be less of a man now.

By staying, refusing to face his fears, he'd be worthless to himself and to Sunny.

"No, sweetheart," he said, saying the same thing he'd told her so many years before, "I have to go."

"Somebody ought to teach you how to tell fibs. You'd get further."

Her petticoat swishing under her calico skirt, she walked in front of him through the door. Why hadn't he kept his mouth shut? she wondered. At least that way she'd be able to live on the belief that maybe, just *maybe*, he'd stay. Why couldn't he ever take the easy roads in life?

She'd have to match his inner strength. He was leaving; she was staying. She had to face it. He could play around, acting as though he were humble and repentant, but he'd made his intentions crystal clear. Bold as brass, he'd returned, knowing there wasn't a child, demanding she owed him what he'd paid for in advance.

Child or no child, she also knew she wanted him. She felt as if she were about to catch fire when she was within three feet of him. Her stomach tightened into love knots. Her hands itched to hold his strong, hard body.

Confronted with that knowledge, she laced her fingers through his. She'd grab him, hold him preciously close, knowing the few moments she had with him were passing swiftly. Some women had a lifetime of love; others had to settle for days, weeks, maybe months if they were lucky.

Short and sweet, she promised silently. There would be no promises, no unspoken lies, no tears or recriminations. She'd have sweet memories of love and laughter to remember long after Blayne had gone.

Blayne watched the play of emotions across Sunny's face, trying to figure out what was going on in her mind. She frowned and worried her lip with her teeth as she stared sightlessly at the sidewalk. Her finger danced across his knuckles. He waited to see if the frown would deepen, knowing that would indicate an unfavorable decision.

She was seated beside him inside the car he'd rented when she came to her decision. Grinning, at peace with herself for a moment, she gave him directions to the restaurant. Quite naturally her hand rested above his knee as he drove in silence.

Friendly silence, Blayne mused, elated to see her smile. Later, after the loving, he'd explain to her why he had to leave. He allowed himself to daydream of Sunny agreeing to stay with him forever. With her hand held tightly in his, they could confront their mutual fear, freeing both of them. He'd aged, but he wasn't too old to dream.

"Six Forks Road," she directed, her hand indicating the direction they should take.

"I've heard north Raleigh should be renamed Yuppie-ville," Blayne teased.

Sunny nodded, chuckling. "You heard right. The locals are outnumbered five to one, but the newcomers are welcome here. Most of them are energetic, talented professionals breathing new life into the area. A few of them are locals who'd left seeking greener pastures and returned."

Blayne volleyed the ball back into her court, "Let's hope the old hometown doesn't turn into one of those cities that's fun to visit but where no one would want to live."

"It won't."

"So speaks the eternal optimist," he chided affectionately. "Five-o'clock traffic is heavier than it used to be."

"Hustle and bustle. I love it."

"And everyone. And everything. You're older, prettier, but—"

"Thanks," Sunny interrupted. Not wanting to hear his stipulation, she flattered herself by adding, "Wiser, too. I've learned to roll with the punches and bend with the wind."

Her fingers closed a bit tighter on his leg, communicating through touch her decision to accept his upcoming departure and not let it inhibit her joy at having him home temporarily. His hand dropped from the steering wheel and covered hers.

"I'll give you an hour to stop playing with my leg," he said lightly. He brought her hand to his lips, which brushed against her knuckles. "I was afraid you'd consider me a bad penny tossed on your doorstep," he confessed. Hand still covering hers, he replaced it on his knee.

She kissed his smooth-shaven cheek. "Never. You're always welcome at home."

"What would you have done if I'd shown up unannounced?" he inquired, thinking he'd have been much smarter not to have sent the telegram.

Mulling the question over in her mind, she replied flippantly, "Passed out in the middle of the floor."

Blayne grimaced. "Damn. I could have given you mouth-to-mouth resuscitation, then carried you off to my lair! Poor planning on my part."

"Better yet, you could have hand-delivered the telegram. Believe me, I was gasping for air when I read it." Noticing they were close to their destination, she added, "After the next stop light, the Peachtree Restaurant is on the right."

"I'm curious about something," he admitted. "Since neither of us has red hair, what made you choose Randy?"

"Availability. Both of Starr's children have red hair."

The twinkle in her blue eyes told him there was a whole lot more she wasn't telling. "And?"

"Creative revenge." Laughter and a groan mixed together. "Explanations require a stiff drink in a public place."

"Why?"

"Because you aren't the type to make a scene in public," she replied wryly.

"Another boner?" he asked, recalling what Sunny called her muddled plans that went astray.

"Big boner," Sunny confirmed, nodding her head. "But I had help this time."

"Starr?"

"Of course. She's an expert at creative revenge. She's been practicing on Joe."

Blayne spotted the sign in front of the restaurant, turned into the parking lot and parked the car. As he helped Sunny from the car he said, "I thought you'd had help with this scheme."

"Why?" She took his arm and walked with him. "You always accused me of getting involved in half-baked ideas."

His arm brushing against the fullness of her breast, combined with the memories of saving Sunny from a million-and-one escapades, made his heart lurch. Errant curls framed her pixie face. She was breathtakingly beautiful. Knowing that soon he'd have to leave her pained him. He had to change her mind one way or another, for both their sakes.

"It just seemed to have the mark of your sister," he replied in answer to her question. "Your schemes were always more impulsive and less elaborate."

Sunny laughed quietly. Her impulsiveness had been the creative spark behind the idea, but Starr had been the one to transform her half-baked idea into a scheme. "You and Starr are both so logical. It's a shame she's still in love with Joe. You'd make a great twosome."

"I'm beginning to think logic and love are a contradiction of terms."

Wondering exactly what he meant, Sunny preceded him into the restaurant.

"Sunny, good to see you," Keith said, advancing toward them. He shifted the leather-bound menus beneath his arm and extended his hand toward Blayne as she made introductions. Keith hugged Sunny affectionately.

While they talked Blayne tried to analyze what Sunny had that made people want to get closer. He used to think it was because wherever she was something was likely to happen; she was sort of a walking bottle rocket. She'd certainly added excitement to his humdrum childhood. Men talked about sex appeal or charisma. He'd met other women who'd been described as charismatic, bright, witty, fun. And yet they were different from Sunny. There was something undefinable about her that made her unforgettable.

If I could bottle it I'd make my first million, Blayne thought, following Keith and Sunny to a secluded table toward the back of the dining room.

"Enjoy yourselves," Keith told them as he returned to his station.

Sunny glanced around the room, which was decorated in deep green and pink from the ceiling to carpet. Beveled mirrors and marble pillars divided the area into cozy corners. A pianist at the baby grand piano added to the congenial atmosphere. "Isn't this chic?"

"Chic," he agreed, dutifully impressed. "What stiff drink would you like? A Tom Collins?"

"Stronger. Straight something or another."

"Straight up or on the rocks?" Amusement lit his eyes. Sunny was the only person he knew who could tell one cola drink from another. Spoiling a Coke by adding liquor was tantamount to committing a sacrilegious act as far as she was concerned. "Single or a double?"

"Wise guy. I'll have a martini with a twist on the rocks." She flashed him a smug smile. Where'd he think she'd been living? In a box? She really didn't like martinis at all, but they suited the sophisticated image she wished to create.

Blayne's blond eyebrow raised skeptically. "Heavy-duty. Wouldn't you prefer to share a bottle of white wine?"

"No, thanks." The waiter approaching the table drew her attention. "Hi, Mark," Sunny called to him.

"Ms. Peiper, how nice to see you." He grinned appreciatively at her colonial-style dress. "It's been a while."

Old home week, Blayne mused, once again noting how the young waiter was drawn to Sunny. Was it just an excess of charm? No, something more. He scowled, wishing he could put a label on the personality trait.

"Sir?"

Blayne gave the waiter the drink order, then settled back into his chair. "Tell me about creative revenge."

"According to Starr, plain, old-fashioned revenge means to get even with somebody. Creative revenge gets you one step ahead." Sunny shrugged. Starr would kick her in the back of her Betsy Ross costume for discussing their strategy. To be at least within the spirit of their compromise, Sunny had to avoid bringing up the cashier's check he'd sent. "You can imagine how disappointed I was when Randy introduced himself and you didn't even bat an eye."

Candidly he said, "Revenge seldom works the way a person plans. What goes around, comes around. What if I told you I was here to get revenge, to settle up old debts?"

Her eyes narrowed. Her decision to live for the moment wavered. She absolutely refused to let him believe she would sleep with him to pay a debt. "Any debt I owe you won't be paid in the bedroom."

The waiter placed her martini on the pink-rimmed plate in front of her. Sunny glanced up. Her thanks froze on her lips as she saw the malicious intent on Mark's face. He had heard what she'd said. Another glass balanced precariously on the edge of the small tray.

"Careful," she cautioned, certain the icy drink would be in Blayne's lap within seconds.

"For you, anything," Mark muttered softly, but Blayne heard.

"Thanks," Sunny said, smiling warmly at the waiter.

Waiting until Mark was out of hearing range, Blayne whispered, "I'm not going to win any popularity awards during my visit. First, the cop, and now the waiter."

"Add my name to the list," she warned, "if you continue to sound as though I owe you sexual favors. I'd only consider making love with you if it was what *I* wanted to do."

Blayne reached across the table and took a sip of her martini and silently cursed his decision to use intimidation to hide his vulnerability. In business matters he'd learned to bargain from strength. Weakness and vulnerability were one and the same in the business world, but the world of personal relationships was quite different. He considered changing tactics.

How would she react if he told her he'd been a victim of terrorists? That he'd regained consciousness in the hospital and fully comprehended her desire to remain in the United States? That years of world travel combined with the accident had made him eager to return home, made him afraid to leave again.

She'd be horrified, he decided.

Although he disliked being heavy-handed, he'd set his course. The telegram had guaranteed reentry into her life. His demand for her to give him a child was as harebrained an idea as Sunny and Starr's scheme. But it was too late to change tactics. He couldn't risk scaring her with the whole truth.

"Are you seriously considering this possibility or have you made a decision?"

"You're drinking my martini," she replied evasively. Retrieving her glass, she decided her evasiveness could be construed as an attempt to be coy. Leveling her eyes with his, she said, "I've made my decision."

"Which is?" The deceptive casualness of his voice hid the pounding in his chest.

"I want to be with you while you're here. I love you."

"And when I leave?"

"I'll stay."

Six

There are some advantages to Raleigh's growth rate," Blayne commented as he opened the door to his hotel room. Sunny led the way inside. "Anonymity. You didn't see anyone in the lobby you recognized, did you?"

"I sure did. I'm just hoping they didn't see me," she mouthed self-consciously. There must have been a meeting of the downtown shop owners that she'd forgotten about. Conspicuously dressed in her colonial costume, she was certain someone had noticed her. She assumed a careless pose and said with feigned sophistication. "Who cares whether or not we were seen? I'm hardly under the age of consent."

Blayne paused inside the threshold, watching as she carelessly kicked off her shoes, wiggled her toes in the thick carpet, then turned toward him. Despite her offhanded reply he could tell she was ill at ease. Motel rooms weren't her style. He'd made a strategical error.

"Something wrong?" she asked, unable to interpret the troubled look he was giving her. He appeared ready to grab her hand and hastily bolt from the room. Didn't he find her attractive anymore? Her fingers nervously toyed with the fabric of her skirt.

Doubts plagued her. What if he'd built her up in his imagination and was finding reality less appealing? What if he wanted her to leave, but didn't want to hurt her feelings? What if . . .

"Nothing that can't be fixed," Blayne said. "Put your shoes on. I'll take you home."

Disappointment slammed through her. She felt like a Christmas package returned to the sender with WRONG ADDRESS stamped on the front. "Men aren't supposed to change their minds. That's a woman's prerogative."

"I haven't changed my mind about loving you or wanting you. But you haven't said ten words since we left the restaurant, and you ran through the lobby like your petticoat was on fire. You're feeling edgy, aren't you?"

Sunny shook her head, realizing she wasn't the only one having an anxiety attack. Unaware of the provocative, gentle sway of her hips as she approached him or of the love shining from her blue eyes, she laid her hand on the front of his shirt.

"It's been forever since we've been together. I guess I'm a little nervous about competing with a memory. What if..."

Her pause and the way her front teeth worried her bottom lip gave Blayne insight into her concern. "What if we aren't physically compatible?"

"Yeah. Something like that." She rested her cheek on his chest when he pulled her snugly against him. A creeping weakness invaded her bones. Supported only by his towering strength, she whispered, "After traveling thousands of miles, your expectations must be high. I'd hate to disappoint you."

Blayne nuzzled his nose in the clean softness of her dark hair. Eyes closing, he stroked her back, shifting his weight to his stronger leg. "Would it comfort you to know I'm suffering from the same pangs of doubt?"

"You? Never. You've always been solid as a rock. When grandfather died and I was beyond the point where words could soothe me, you came to me. You're the one who took a teary-eyed adolescent and made her smile again."

Blayne remembered everything about the most memorable night in his life. He'd come to her as a friend and left as her lover. "I had the best of intentions."

"After midnight? When 'all the hellin' in the world goes on'?" she asked, quoting her grandfather.

"I only intended to hold you until you quit crying and drifted off to sleep." His fingers twined through her hair. "How was I to know you slept without a nightgown?"

Her lips curved into a gentle smile of remembrance. "Why did you think I wouldn't get out from under the bedcovers when I saw you crawl through the window?"

"You were cold?"

"In August?"

"Truth be known, I was too distraught from seeing your red eyes and shuffling walk to notice anything. I didn't know what I was doing. All I did know was that I had to make everything right for you."

"You did. Beautifully." Her arm curved around his shoulder. "You gave me love."

Grinning sardonically, Blayne mumbled, "I gave you inexperience, fumbling."

"Both of us fumbled. Neither one of us had gone beyond light caresses. Maybe that's what made it so right."

"You made me feel ten feet tall. I didn't think I'd be able to crawl back through the window."

He lightly peppered kisses into her hair. Beneath her hand she felt his strong heartbeat. His hands slid down her spine until they rested low on her hips.

"We couldn't look each other in the face the next day," she remembered.

"Hmmmm. I thought you hated me for taking advantage of you."

"I seem to recall being the one to pull you between the sheets." Ever so gently his pelvis rocked from side to side against her. She tilted her head backward. "You proposed."

"You laughed."

"Nervous reaction," Sunny said apologetically. "We were both too young and inexperienced. You had those dreams of faraway places. I loved you enough to know I had to let you find happiness without me."

Blayne realized they were on dangerous ground. One wrong response and she'd flee. Thank God she hadn't been with him at the airport when the bomb exploded. She could have been killed. His eyes moistened, shimmering in the lamplight. "I counted on your loving me enough to come with me," he replied, voice husky with emotion.

"When you left I discovered how weak I really was. I'd rehearsed in my mind how I was going to be dry-eyed, bravely smiling and waving goodbye." Her breath caught in her throat. Her hand fluttered aimlessly across his shoulder blades. "I disgraced myself by bawling so damned hard I couldn't think straight. You were being so stoic, so honorable, so kind, and I was acting like a selfish, spoiled brat who was throwing a tantrum because she couldn't have what she wanted."

"Selfish? You?" His lips barely touched hers. "Never."

"I had this rotten premonition that something terrible would happen to you . . . like it did to my parents. Fear and desperation made me a coward when I wanted to be courageous.''

He framed her face with his hands. Her eyes glowed with long-suppressed fear. "I'm home, sweetheart. Safe."

She stood on tiptoe and locked her arms around his neck. "Love me, Blayne. Please?"

All awkwardness disappeared. She kissed him with all the pent-up fervor she'd saved for him. Under his touch her body became pliant. She floated dizzily as he swung her into his arms. His unsteady gait made her certain he was deeply affected by what she'd told him.

Blayne stumbled, lunging toward the bed. Inwardly he cursed his impaired knee. Recovering his balance, with painstaking slowness, he lowered her to the bed. Reaching toward the nightstand, he turned off the light. He knew the sight of his damaged leg would make her ask questions he preferred to delay answering.

His lips closed over hers to still the protest he saw forming. He lay down beside her, cherishing her with his love. Lips closed, he delayed kissing her. Age and experience had taught him that mutual anticipation guaranteed total fulfillment.

Much as he wanted to bury himself deep inside her, he wanted her to reach such a charged state of arousal she couldn't bear to say no.

Resistance was the magical key.

Sunny parted her lips, impatient with the teasing flicks of his tongue. His lips nibbled, sipped, thoroughly arousing her. Although impulsive, occasionally reckless, she'd never before taken the initiative, but this time her tongue darted boldly between his lips. Tentatively, his tongue welcomed her, then resisted by withdrawing, teasing, seducing, beckoning her to explore.

His fingers traced the vee of her neckline and fingered the cloth-covered buttons—without opening them. He touched her through the layers of fabric and she arched against his hand.

Small unrecognizable sounds formed deep within Sunny as uncertainty formed in her mind. Blayne had touched her like this when he'd known they couldn't consummate their love. His iron will forged boundaries he wouldn't cross.

"Blayne," she pleaded against his lips, "kiss me properly."

With agonizing slowness his velvet soft tongue stroked her. Silently he told her their making love completely had to be her choice. Exquisite torment, she thought, eager to be one with him.

She nimbly unbuttoned his shirt and pulled it from the waistband of his pants. Blayne shrugged his shoulders, which allowed her to remove it, to heedlessly cast his shirt to the floor.

Sunny rubbed her cheek against his chest hairs. Her fingers followed the indentation of his back. His shoulders were broad, far more muscular than they had been when he'd been a younger man. Her petticoat and skirt bunched to her knees as her leg twined behind his knee, drawing him between her legs. She felt her breasts grow taut, her nipples harden in the confinement of her bra.

Resist, resist, Blayne coached himself, feeling her strain against him.

He lowered his lips to the hollow of her collarbone. His senses flamed with pounding need. And yet he continued slowly, anticipating the treasure beneath the yards of encumbering fabric. As if in slow motion, he unbuttoned her dress without opening it. In the darkness, his hand felt a tiny drawstring ribbon lacing her petticoat together. His jaw clenched in reaction to the thought of baring her breasts.

Soon, he promised, soon he'd permit himself to touch her.

Impatient for his touch, Sunny agilely removed the top of her dress. Her arms tightened, pulling his head close. A shiver of passion ran through her as his mouth closed over her cotton slip. His lips and teeth sought and found her nipple, teasing the bud until she thought she'd burst with pleasure.

His hands cupped her breasts, his mouth moving from one turgid peak to the other, driving her to wildness. When she thought she'd resort to ripping the petticoat from her body, she felt his forefinger gingerly unlacing the ribbon. He kissed a delicious path from the valley of her breasts to her waistband. Her fingers wove into his golden hair, and she raised her shoulders from the pillow, thrusting her breasts against the wall of his chest.

She moaned with gratitude when he removed the garment.

"You're lovely...lovely...lovely," he murmured as his thumbs made circular motions around her sensitive nipples. His mouth grew dry. Excitement coursed through him. He wanted to see her. Touch wasn't enough. He knew he could learn to hate the darkness that prohibited him from gazing at her. "I want to taste you," he said, his voice strangling in the back of his throat.

Her eyes squeezed shut, tiny bursts of light exploded in front of her eyes as his lips and tongue gently tugged at her. A tear slid down the side of her face. Mindlessly she twisted closer to him, tugging at the hook and eye attached to her waistband. It finally popped loose, breaking the braided strands of thread holding it together.

Blayne heard the sound. His lips curved as he sluggishly suckled her, delighted with her impatience. Her wiggling from her clothing nearly destroyed his intention to proceed slowly and with caution. Her nakedness threatened to demolish the tight bonds of restraint he'd imposed on himself.

He moved away from her, but kept one hand skimming over her as he removed the remainder of his clothing.

"Blayne?" The sudden awareness that he had gotten off the bed forced her eyes wide open. He couldn't do this to her and leave. She ached from wanting him. Rolling to her side, she reached blindly into the darkness.

"I'm here, sweetheart," he murmured. His slacks and briefs fell to the floor as he stood beside the bed.

His hand lowered below her waist to caress her thighs. Her knees bent, and she drew toward him.

The slender thread of light coming from beneath the door behind Blayne made him appear like a huge shadow. She'd dreamt of him too often to be satisfied with her sense of touch and smell. "Turn on the light," she urged. "I want to see you."

He couldn't. Although he desperately wanted to feast his eyes on her, he couldn't. His wounds were too recent, the scars too visible. Instead of making love, he'd be making explanations.

"Touch me," he offered taking her hand and guiding it across his torso, down his uninjured thigh.

He opened the drawer of the nightstand. Years ago he'd neglected his responsibility by not protecting her. As a young man, he'd excused his negligence the next morning by admitting he was caught in a web of passion. He'd matured past the stage of uncontrollable desire. He was definitely not going to risk an unplanned pregnancy this time.

"I love the feel of your skin," she whispered. "Smooth and supple. Perfect."

Imperfect, Blayne corrected silently, distracting her from turning on the light with long, sensuous strokes from her shoulders to her rounded hips. He returned to her side, fitting their bodies closely together.

Unable to resist any longer, he coaxed her legs apart with a gentle pressure of his hand. "It's all right, sweetheart," he promised when her thigh muscles automatically flexed.

"Come to me," she implored. "Love me."

Her arms encircled his waist; her legs parted to welcome him. She wasn't afraid. His soft reassurance erased all her doubts. Loving Blayne could only be beautiful; it always had been, always would be.

Blayne could wait no longer. He sank into her, muffling a groan of exquisite pleasure against her neck. He was home, finally. And he was making love to the one woman in the world who could make him happy.

With each powerful thrust of his hips, he vowed to keep her with him. She arched and twisted in her passion, but they remained as one in their climb to ecstasy. He led her to the limit of her desire and beyond, then he followed her into uncharted territory. His husky whispers were in the language of love, incomprehensible and foreign to anyone other than the two of them.

Sunny understood him. His disjointed phrases encouraged her to go with him, not to hold back. She wasn't afraid. She was sheltered in his tenderness and love and knew Blayne would keep both of them safe.

He held her close to his heart, savoring the profound sense of satisfaction flooding through him. After long moments she stirred in his arms. He shifted his weight to the side of her and pulled the coverlet at the foot of the bed over both of them.

Smiling, Sunny wondered if Blayne had been as deeply affected as she'd been. She huddled next to him, clinging to the last vestige of the afterglow. Making love with Blayne was like Christmas and the Fourth of July all rolled into one.

Blayne kissed her forehead, then folded the pillow and propped it under his head. He traced her smile with one finger. "What are you thinking?"

"Silly thoughts," she blurted.

"Such as?"

"Fireworks, Christmas candles, brilliant sparks of red, green, white and blue." She stretched languorously, then curled against him. "Silly things."

"Any doubts remaining about pleasing me?"

"Did I?"

Blayne chuckled and brushed a damp strand of hair away from her face. "Immeasurably."

"Ditto." Her smile reflected her smugness. "Double ditto."

"You used to be more talkative."

"Complaining?"

"I wouldn't mind hearing an avowal of undying love," he joked half-seriously.

"Careful," she warned, rolling onto her back, "you're contradicting yourself. Earlier today you criticized me for saying I loved everything."

Laughing softly, Blayne said, "It's tough on my self-esteem wondering whether you love home-canned food more than you love me."

"I love you more than pickled beets," she affirmed, saucily adding, "but decorated Christmas trees? That would put you into some tough competition."

"Thanks a bunch," he said, sighing. "You're supposed to be gushing love talk, and you compare me with a prickly pine tree."

She caressed the whiskers on his chin. "I'd say you're a mite prickly. You smell good, too."

"Terrific! Want me to don some colored lights and stand in front of the window?"

"I have a better idea." She snuggled against him under the coverlet. "Why don't we celebrate Christmas in July by your giving me the best present in the world."

"What's that?"

Sunny was tempted to ask him to promise to be with her on December twenty-fifth, but she wouldn't ask for the impossible. "Love me."

"I do love you, sweetheart," he replied, pretending he didn't understand her meaning. "*More* than pickled beets and Christmas trees."

"More than the bright lights of Cairo and Paris?" Sunny voiced her thoughts before she'd considered how he'd respond. Certain she didn't want to hear the answer, she silenced him by placing her fingers over his mouth. "I love you, Blayne."

He kissed each finger with loving care. "Enough to marry me?"

"Blayne, we went through this seven years ago. I'm reconciled to the fact that you'll be leaving. Don't ask for more."

"I want more than a brief affair. I want you . . . a child like Randy . . . a family. I've been away, but I've never forgotten you. Don't you realize I've loved you for so long, I don't remember what it was like not to love you? You're a vital part of me."

"Stop, please," she begged. How often had she yearned to hear him say those exact words? And yet, once he'd voiced them, they brought tears to her eyes. "You're making this hard for both of us."

"Nothing worthwhile comes easy. We've both had to work hard for everything we have." Her head shaking stubbornly back and forth against his chest told him that he hadn't convinced her. "Go with me . . . just once," he urged.

"No. I have a business here, a life I've made for myself."

Blayne stilled her head by placing his hand on her nape. His thumb lazily soothed her stiff neck muscles. She was silently fighting him. He'd won one major victory since returning home. He wondered if he should take a chance on pushing her toward his predetermined goal. With her in his arms, he decided to push his advantage.

"Sunny, wouldn't you enjoy meeting the woodcarver who made the Black Forest clocks lining the back of your shop? What about the boxes of hand-blown glass Christmas ornaments from Belgium that I saw in the corner? Aren't you curious about your craftsmen?"

"We exchange letters, pictures and an occasional phone call. Peter Krantz does the woodwork on the clocks. He's forty-two, married and has four children. Aside from making clocks, he has a part-time job selling bicycles. Want to hear about Karl? He's the glassblower."

She refused to acknowledge the limitations of her life in Raleigh, but she couldn't help imagining watching a master artisan like Karl as he worked at his craft.

Each year when she'd unpacked the Royal Copenhagen Christmas Plates, she'd wondered how the blue underglaze was applied to the fine porcelain. There were other items in the Holiday Shoppe Blayne hadn't noticed: Crummel boxes and Doulton figurines from England, gourmet foods from France, wooden and wax ornaments from Germany. All had been created by experts who were eager to demonstrate their craft.

Between specific holidays she stocked the shop with hand-knitted sweaters from Scotland, England and Peru. Her armchair travels took her beyond Europe to South America, Africa, Japan, Australia and the Middle East. Al, the postman, was constantly amazed by the variety of stamps she'd collected to give to his mother.

"After the Fourth, there aren't any holidays until Labor Day. It's a slack time at the store, isn't it?"

She knew what he was going to say next: You aren't busy; you can come with me. She rolled onto her back and stared at the ceiling.

"I'm busy ordering for Christmas."

"Go with me," Blayne coaxed. "I promise to take you to watch Peter and Karl work. We'll meet with all your suppliers."

The nagging fear she'd felt since she was a child made her hands tremble as she nervously pleated the coverlet between her fingers. Right now, in the safety of Blayne's bed, she could feel adrenaline beginning to pump through her system. She could still visualize the day her parents had been killed, remember desperately running to search for them. Her throat tightened from the memory of screaming until only pitiful whimpers squeezed from her throat.

She kept her eyes open. Her lips moved soundlessly as she repeated the vow she'd made. *I'll never leave the United States.*

"Sunny?" Concerned by her silence, Blayne moved closer.

"I can't."

Blayne heard the finality in her succinct response. He realized where her thoughts had taken her. Cradling her into his arms, he rocked her gently. "You have to bury the past."

"I have. But I'm not going to cut short my future," she replied with as much levity as she could muster.

"Do you think I'd take you to a war-torn country in the middle of a revolution? I'm not crazy."

"Neither am I. Don't you read the newspapers? Hundreds of would-be tourists canceled their reservations this summer. I'm not the only American staying at home. Frankly, I hate the idea of traveling with an American passport. In some countries that makes you a target for every maniac with a political grudge."

Certain he was losing, Blayne tried another tactic. "Danger exists everywhere."

"The mayor and the city council may have a few tiffs, but they don't pull out their guns and start shooting at each other," she argued.

"No street crime? No accidents? Much as I love my hometown, it isn't Utopia. I know you have good reason for your fears, but staying in a rut doesn't guarantee safety. Besides, many parts of the world are as safe as the U.S.A., if not safer."

"Maybe," she answered. "But I'm happy here. It's perfect for me." She turned her face toward him. While he'd been trying to convince her to travel with him, she'd been mulling over the idea of convincing him to stay. Raleigh had changed. Locals were no longer forced to leave the area for high-tech employment. There were now many firms that could offer a good job to a man with his expertise. "It could be perfect for you, too."

"I recall you and Starr arguing, until I thought you were going to kill each other, and shouting 'Compromise.' Would you be willing to compromise with me?"

She felt a flutter inside her. "I'm still recovering from the last compromise Starr negotiated. You two always manage to twist my mind until it resembles a pretzel."

"No mind-twist or hammer-hold arm locks," he promised. "A straightforward, aboveboard deal."

"Let's hear it."

"I'll put in my application with local companies if you'll go with me on my next assignment abroad."

"Where is your next assignment?" she asked suspiciously, wanting to know the details before considering the compromise.

"I don't know, yet. But I should be hearing in the next couple of days."

"Would we be leaving immediately? Before the Fourth of July?"

"Possibly."

"Can I have time to think over your offer?"

Blayne considered giving her to the count of ten. Impulsively, she might give him a quick yes. If she had a few days to think she'd probably worry herself into a tizzy. But then again, it wasn't fair to ask her to go with him if he didn't even know where he was going. Once he learned his destination, he might decide it was too dangerous for her to accompany him.

"We both need to know where we'd be going. How about twenty-four hours after I'm called? Is that agreeable?"

Sunny paused thoughtfully. "That isn't much time to make arrangements."

"I can take care of the details. All you have to do is say yes."

"I'm only agreeing to think about it," she said. "Right?"

"For now."

"What if I put out a few feelers with local companies and you're offered a job too good to refuse?" she asked, searching for a loophole in the compromise. Energized by the thought of Blayne's agreeing to return permanently, she hugged him enthusiastically. "I know plenty of businessmen who'd jump at the chance to employ you.''

"Forget it, Sunny. Our honeymoon comes first.''

"What if . . .''

"No more 'what ifs,' '' Blayne said, kissing her gently.

"But, Blayne, you could miss the job opportunity of a lifetime with your bullheadedness. A prospective employer isn't going to twiddle his thumbs waiting for you to complete another assignment.''

He grinned. Money was the last of his worries. The majority of his paychecks were safely banked. He wasn't rich, but they could live comfortably on his savings for quite a while. Certain Sunny was concerned about her ability to support him should he become unemployed, he said, "No problem, love. I won't live off of the income from the Holiday Shoppe. If worse comes to worse, we can always live for a while on the money I sent you.''

"But . . .'' *I don't have all the money!* Her last avenue of escape disappeared. Mind whirling from the effect of his hands that were stroking her sensuously, she groaned in frustration. "We've got to talk.''

Blayne cupped her full breast in one hand. The dark nipple immediately puckered in response. "Body language can say it all, sweetheart. Let me feel how much you love me.''

Seven

A sliver of sunshine coming through the closed drapes awakened Sunny. Blayne's arm circled her waist, possessively holding their satiated bodies together spoon-fashion. Sunny blinked the last vestiges of sleep from her eyes as she yawned.

Careful not to wake him, she cautiously slid his arm aside and slipped from the bed. On tiptoe she went into the bathroom. A quick glance into the mirror brought a wide smile to her lips. The sandpaper texture of Blayne's whiskers had left her cheeks a rosy pink.

"Plush," she commented after emptying the contents of a small basket of complimentary toiletries and inspecting them. The bathroom had everything, including a telephone and a brown terry-cloth robe. Deciding to avail herself of the facilities, she used the phone and ordered a giant-sized breakfast. "Nothing so romantic as breakfast in bed," she told her reflection after she had hung up.

By the time she'd finished her shower, dried off and slipped into the robe, she was deep in thought. Glorious though the night had been, Blayne had made it clear that his plans included her going abroad with him. The real kick in the pants was knowing that if she had ever had any real chance of keeping him in North Carolina, she'd probably blown it by spending most of the money he'd sent her.

Why, oh why hadn't she stuck to her resolution not to spend a dime of that money? The first few times she'd dipped into the reserve fund, she'd meticulously replaced it within the month. But with one crisis following another, she'd fallen quite a bit behind. Now, if Blayne decided to stay in Raleigh, he'd need that money until he found gainful employment. If he found out the money wasn't all there, he might have to accept the next foreign assignment he was offered.

Why couldn't he have come home for Christmas? By then she might have been able to replace the money. But no, he'd arrived before she could harvest the trees.

Taking his brush from the leather shaving kit beside the sink, she began brushing her hair in long strokes.

She wondered how Blayne would react to the whole truth. He'd certainly been a good sport about Randy.

Of course, he said he'd known all along she didn't have a child. Knowing in advance made a difference. She'd bet her last dime that he didn't know about the money.

Of course he was aware she had always spent money far too freely, but she felt certain he expected her to have grown out of her frivolous disregard for money. It would take a lot of courage to look Blayne in the eye and say, "Hey, I don't have your fifteen thousand dollars. I don't have your child, either."

Scrupulously honest, she shuddered at her unintentionally unethical behavior. When she borrowed the money she hadn't felt dishonest. What was she supposed to do? Let Starr and the boys starve? Let Randy miss a whole year of school because of his allergies? Let Russell have buck teeth?

The bristle of the brush snarled in her hair as she shook her head. Generous to a flaw, she'd rashly withdrawn money from the special account. Given the same set of circumstances, she'd probably make the same mistake again.

I'll tell him, she thought. *It's the only mature thing to do.*

Her hand shook as she quietly returned the brush to the shaving kit. She dreaded seeing the look of disappointment on Blayne's face. Procrastinating, she gave her hair a final fluff, then whispered to her reflection, "After breakfast."

Silently she entered the faintly lit bedroom. Sound asleep, Blayne lay sprawled on the bed. The sheet had twisted between his muscular thighs, exposing one long leg. She hated the thought of wakening him to give him bad news.

A keen sense of yearning pierced her heart. She silently drew back the draperies to let in light, thus enabling her to watch him sleeping.

Her eyes widened as they followed the curve of his body. Taut, smooth skin stretched across his shoulder, but a network of scarcely healed scars marred his upper thigh, knee and calf.

Her sharp intake of breath woke Blayne. In an instant he saw that she was gazing at his injured leg. Tears pooled in the corners of her eyes and began sliding down her cheeks.

"You were hurt." Her speech slurred and became thick with emotion. "How? When? Where?"

Blayne flinched as she reached out to touch the scarred skin. He shrank from the thought of telling her how he'd been injured. Last night, laying safe in his arms, she'd come close to promising to go with him. At least she'd agreed to consider the idea. Once he answered her questions, he knew her fear would be worse than ever.

Dropping to her knees, Sunny ran her lips down the length of his leg and wished her touch could heal the wound. All thought of telling him about how she'd spent his money disappeared with her concern for his well-being.

Her breathing was ragged as she said, "It must have hurt terribly."

"It's okay, sweetheart," Blayne whispered, touched by her gentleness and her tears.

Sunny felt a sob building in her chest. He'd been severely injured; he could have been permanently crippled. The thought of Blayne losing his leg made Sunny burst into tears again. Her shoulders shook. She wrapped her arms around him, holding on to him for dear life.

Feeling inadequate and helpless against her crying, Blayne scooped her into his arms and held her close. One hand threaded through her dark hair, the other massaged her shoulders and waist.

"I'm all right," he reassured her. "The doctors told me the scars would fade with time."

Her small fist pounded his chest. "I knew something would happen to you," she moaned, hiccupping between phrases. "I knew I should have done everything I could to keep you here. I could have lost you forever."

"You didn't, sweetheart. I'm here. Safe." He futilely tried to find a way to stop her tears. Hoping her sense of humor would rescue her, he added, "I'm too ornery to die."

Sunny dug her nails into his shoulders, shaking him. In a moment of atypical selfishness she sobbed, "Don't make light of my fears. How do you think I would have felt if I'd read in the newspaper that you'd been killed? I'd have died inch by inch knowing I'd never see you again."

"Don't think about it," he whispered close to her ear.

"I can't help it. It scares me."

A sharp rap at the door brought Sunny to her feet. She pulled a tissue from the box on the night table and wiped her eyes. Her chin trembled as she said, "I ordered breakfast."

"Forget breakfast. I'll get rid of him." Blayne started to spring from the bed, but his knee stiffened. His heart ached when he saw a fresh deluge of tears streaming down Sunny's face. In a tone that was sharper than he intended, he ordered her to get back into bed. Picking up his slacks, he pulled them on and opened the door.

Sunny obediently crawled under the covers. The sheets were still warm from his body heat. Her imagination ran wild. Blayne was an integral part of her life. She hurt for him.

The bellboy's early morning greeting was more than Blayne could stomach. "I'll take it," he snapped when the young man started across the threshold. His concern for Sunny outweighed his usual good manners. "Put it on the room tab."

He balanced on his good leg and kicked the door shut. As he hobbled to the bed, he cursed himself for not telling Sunny about his leg, rather than letting the harsh morning sunlight illuminate his disfigurement. But when could he have told her? The right moment hadn't arisen.

Sunny saw his grim expression. Each hesitant step he took bruised her tender heart, but she'd decided crying like a two-year-old wasn't a remedy for the pain he suffered. Her voice was quiet when she said, "Tell me about it."

"Airport bombing. The Middle East." He wouldn't embellish the bare facts. She shuddered. He unfolded the tray's legs and placed it on Sunny's lap. "I was in the hospital nearly a month."

She avoided meeting his eyes. The cold facts, curtly stated, chilled her to the bone. Goose bumps covered her shoulders and arms. One thought repeatedly ran through her mind: I can't go with him.

"Sunny, listen to me." Blayne sat on the edge of the bed. "I've been in hot spots for the past seven years. Nothing happened. Just once I was at the wrong place at the wrong time."

"Don't tell me that! You were lucky up until this happened. A cat may have nine lives, but you don't."

"The odds of it happening again are infinitesimally small." He'd used the same logic to convince himself he'd be safe. It hadn't worked for him any more than it worked for Sunny. Blayne shook his head to clear his mind. With undo force he said, "Nothing will happen to us."

Sunny stared down at the breakfast tray to avoid looking into Blayne's eyes. An envelope was tucked between the salt and pepper shakers. Since she was in Blayne's room, the letter had to be for him. As she handed it to him, her heartbeat accelerated. Only his present employer knew where to reach him.

Blayne glanced at the message, picked up the phone and asked for room service.

"What is it?" Sunny asked, baffled. Was he in pain? His face had drained of color.

"Blayne MacCaffrey, room 512. An envelope was on my breakfast tray. Can you tell me how it got there?"

Sunny watched him crumple the sheet of paper into a tight wad. His knuckles turned white as he clenched his fist. "What is it?"

"The bellboy doesn't know? Thank you." Blayne disconnected the line and stood up. "What the hell is going on around here?"

Trapped by the breakfast tray, Sunny held out her hand. "Is it from your boss?"

Blayne considered tossing the paper into the waste can and making some insipid excuse, but he knew Sunny was too perceptive for such a ploy. He smoothed the page and handed it to her.

Printed block letters cut from magazines and newspapers formed the words: "You're gonna get it. Stay away from..." A picture of a brilliant sunset concluded the message.

Sunny swallowed. "Who'd send this?"

"You tell me. Do you have some jealous boyfriend around who wants to get rid of me?"

She reread the note, then handed him the tray. Her hands shook so badly she spilled some of her coffee. "You know better. Could it be a prank?"

"Starr," Blayne said suddenly. "She'd do something crazy like this if she thought you were going to leave with me."

"Don't be silly. My sister might give you a face-to-face tongue-lashing, but she'd never send an anonymous letter."

"Who else knows that I'm here? I haven't contacted anyone beside you and Starr. It has to be your sister."

Angry, Sunny whipped back the bedcovers, picked up her clothes and headed for the bathroom. "Starr wouldn't openly threaten you. Creative revenge is more to her taste. You don't even know you've been zapped until you hear her laughing. I'm going to get dressed and go straight to her house."

"I'm coming with you."

Blayne had been in tight corners where danger lurked behind every door, but the thought of someone threatening him in his own hometown appalled him. He grabbed a shirt from the closet, hastily put it on, then zipped up his carryall bag and laid it on the bed.

From behind the closed door Sunny answered, "Pack your bags. You can stay at my condo. I'm not taking any chances on letting anything happen to you while you're here."

Dressed in the clothing she'd worn the previous day, Sunny hurried from the bathroom to the telephone. "You may be right," she finally agreed. "Starr's crazy, mixed-up logic may have led her to paste together that note. I'm going to call her while you shave."

"She didn't know where I was staying, did she?"

Blayne stepped into the bathroom. He heated his shaving brush by running it under hot water as he put a new blade in his razor.

"I don't know, but it wouldn't be too difficult to find out," Sunny shouted over the sound of splashing water.

She dialed Starr's number. Her sister might have called her at home late last night to see if Sunny had stuck to their compromise agreement. When no one answered the phone, Starr could have assumed she was with Blayne. One assumption would have led to another, which could have resulted in Starr's deciding to get a little creative revenge on both Blayne and her sister.

Sunny mentally analyzed the note from Starr's viewpoint. "You're gonna get it" could refer to the money. "Stay away from the sunset" could mean don't be with Sunny after dark. The entire tone of the message could be different from how Blayne interpreted it.

"Randy? Is your mom home?"

"Hi, Aunt Sunny! Nope, she went to get donuts, but she'll be right back."

"When she gets home, tell her to stay there. I need to talk to her."

"Are you going to bring Mr. MacCaffrey with you? He said he'd play Froggie with me."

"Yes, dear, he's coming with me." Anticipating Randy's exuberant reaction, she moved the receiver away from her ear.

"Yea!" Randy shouted.

"By the way, did your mom call me last night?"

"I don't think so. Dad was here, and they went for a long ride." His voice lowered. "I'm gonna get my Christmas wish. I can tell."

"We'll see," she replied cautiously. "Make certain your mom stays home until I get there. Okay?"

"Okay. See you soon."

"Bye."

Sunny returned the receiver to its cradle. Starr wasn't at home. She could have told the boys she was going after donuts and driven to the hotel. Inwardly groaning at the possibility of Starr having left the note, Sunny stood and crossed to the window. Her sister's main objective was to get Blayne out of town without repaying him. Surely Starr didn't think the note would accomplish that. Deep down, Sunny's instincts told her Starr hadn't sent the message despite her wanting Blayne to leave.

Then who sent it? She pondered the question but couldn't come up with another name.

She turned toward the bathroom. "Doesn't the company you're working for know where you're staying?"

"Yeah. But *Fortune* 500 companies usually don't paste together threatening letters."

"You aren't involved in anything like espionage, are you?" The idea was farfetched but not inconceivable. After all, Blayne had been moving from one foreign country to the next for years. His being a computer whiz would be a perfect cover. The thought of Blayne being a spy of some kind sent shivers down her spine.

"Your imagination is working overtime, sweet-heart. I'm an American businessman, not a CIA spy."

"On television, that's what all the spies say."

Blayne wiped the residue of lather from his face, tossed the towel on the side of the bathtub, closed his shaving kit and strode into the bedroom. "Believe me, Sunny, I'm not spy material."

"Well, I can't believe Starr would send a threatening letter, either."

"Frankly, neither can I, but we'll talk to her just to make certain."

He gathered his belongings and opened the door. "I'll check out, then meet you at the car. To be on the safe side I don't think you should be too close to me."

"You aren't going anywhere without me, mister. Two sets of eyes are better than one." She took hold of his arm, refusing to let him go alone.

"Sunny, I'm not going to hide behind your petticoats, and I'm not going to let anything happen to you. For once in your life, do what I tell you to do!"

As he punched the elevator button, another thought occurred to him. Could the note have been sent to Sunny?

"You don't have any enemies, do you?" he asked, striving to sound nonchalant. He didn't want to alarm her, but the note made more sense if she were the recipient.

His casual inquiry didn't fool Sunny. "You don't think that note was meant for me, do you?"

He watched her look from his face to down the deserted corridor. Sorry he'd even mentioned the possibility, he laced his fingers through hers. "No one would want to hurt you," he said reassuringly.

"Now wait a minute. Last week I saw a television program where an importer received a shipment that contained stolen Egyptian artifacts. I have crates of unopened shipments in the storage room. Maybe—"

"Sweetheart, you're letting your imagination run wild." Although his voice was calm, his insides were twisting. She could be right. Sweet, innocent, generous Sunny was the perfect recipient for an illicit shipment. Her explanation made at least as much sense as accusing Starr. "I'll tell you what, I'll drop you off at Starr's house. While you talk to her, I'll check out your storage room."

"No way! I'm calling the police."

"Your policeman friend already dislikes me. You call him and he'll arrest me."

"For what?"

"Who knows. He's just looking for an excuse."

The bell over the elevator door rang, and the steel doors parted. Both Sunny and Blayne held their breath. Blayne stepped protectively in front of Sunny as a muscular man dressed in a navy blue pin-striped suit walked out of the elevator toward them.

"Morning," the stranger said cheerfully.

Blayne and Sunny replied in unison, "Morning," and hurried into the elevator. Realizing they'd both come to the same erroneous conclusion about the friendly stranger, Sunny chuckled.

"Who has a wild imagination?" she asked wryly.

"We're both getting fanciful. You have to admit though, he did look like Al Capone's right-hand man."

The elevator's swift decent had Sunny's stomach competing for space in her rib cage.

"You're going with me to the front desk," Blayne ordered, changing his original plan. "I'm not letting you out of my sight until you're safely at your sister's house."

"Blayne, you do think they're after me, don't you?"

"I'm not taking chances. Somebody came in the back door of your shop yesterday while we were out front."

"Why would someone sneak through the back door intent on mischief and leave a five-dollar bill beside the cash register? That doesn't make a bit of sense."

It didn't make sense to Blayne, either, but he wasn't taking any chances when Sunny's life could be at risk. "I didn't major in criminology. How should I know how a crook thinks?"

"I'm going to call the police," she stated firmly.

The elevator door opened, and Blayne pulled Sunny backward against him.

"Damn it, woman, stay beside me." He looked outside and said, "All clear. You are not going to call your friend. How the heck am I going to protect you if I'm locked up in jail?"

"I'll tell him you aren't involved," she protested. "Or I won't ask for him."

"Believe me, he'll be the one to answer the call. For once in your life you're going to do things my way. Understand?"

The desk clerk turned from the pigeonhole mail slots. "Checking out?"

"Yes," Blayne replied, pushing the key across the marble desktop. He picked up a pen. "What's Starr's phone number? I'll have my business calls transferred to her house."

Giving Blayne a dirty look, she told him the number. "I'm not some nitwit you can order around like you did when we were kids," she said angrily.

Blayne laughed sharply but without humor. "You've never taken orders from me," he replied in a quiet voice for her ears only.

"Well, I'm too old to start now." She glanced from side to side and around the perimeter of the lobby. "The note had to be to you. Nothing like this ever happened in Raleigh until you arrived here."

Disregarding her words, Blayne signed the credit card slip. "Forward any calls to this number," he told the desk clerk.

Turning on his heel, he grasped Sunny by the elbow and hustled her toward the door. The clerk barely had time to recite his departure spiel before they were gone.

"Slow down," she panted, yanking her long skirt up until her frilly pantaloons gave her the freedom to keep pace with him. She'd noticed he had begun to limp heavily, and rather than point out his handicap, she added, "Aren't we supposed to be zigzagging?"

Blayne stopped beside the rental car and unlocked the door for her. "Get in."

While he stowed his carryall in the trunk, she smiled. She knew Blayne was the masterful type, and she liked the idea of his protecting her from evil forces. Of course Starr would accuse her of being melodramatic, but she didn't care. The thought of Blayne risking himself to protect her from danger was decidedly exhilarating.

"Where does Starr live?" Blayne asked as he started the engine.

"In Granddad's house. She needed the extra space for the boys."

"It's a shame I no longer own the house I grew up in. You could stay with Starr until this is settled and I could be right next door."

Sunny, the perpetual optimist, grinned and winked. "I'm glad you don't. This way we have privacy. You have to stay with me at my place."

"You have a knack for finding something good in a bad situation."

"Are you complaining?"

Unwillingly Blayne returned her smile. "Sweetheart, the thought of staying close to you has great appeal."

His right hand strayed from the steering wheel long enough to caress her knee. He thought of another positive aspect of their current situation. Sunny would have to admit that danger could occur anywhere, even in Raleigh. Later, when they'd solved the mystery of the anonymous note, he'd remind her of that fact.

An odd thought struck Sunny. She shifted in her seat, staring at Blayne. Could he have arranged to have the note sent to his room? He'd told her yesterday that being safe was a state of mind; danger could be found anywhere.

No, Blayne wouldn't frighten her to prove his point. Remembering how he'd reacted, she discarded the wild idea. But if Starr hadn't sent the note, and Blayne hadn't, who had? And for whom was the note intended?

She frowned in consternation. There had to be a simple explanation.

"Blayne," she said thoughtfully, "neither of our names was on the envelope. Do you think someone was pulling a prank and the message was sent to the wrong room?"

He shrugged. "It's feasible. You don't have any enemies; I don't have any. There must be a mix-up of some sort, but I'd rather be safe than sorry."

"Can I get that in writing?"

"Why?"

"Because your statement demolishes your reasons for traveling, especially considering your wounded leg."

Chuckling, Blayne glanced at the smug smile on Sunny's face. "Careful. You're going to make me wonder if you sent the message."

"Why would I send it?"

"You know I'm a mystery buff. Perhaps you think you can string this one out for say...oh, the next ten to twenty years. I can see you rocking in a granny chair and finally admitting you sent the note.''

"I wouldn't do something like that, even to keep you in Raleigh,'' she said, protesting her innocence. She blushed as she recalled what she'd done the last time he'd told her he was leaving. From the way his blond eyebrow was arched, she knew Blayne was recalling the incident also. "'I *could* be pregnant,' that's what I said, not I *am* pregnant. As soon as I knew for certain I wasn't, I wrote to you.''

"I'd say my telegram evened the score,'' he replied. "My reasons for accepting the next assignment aren't the same ones I had years ago.''

"Oh? Then why are you going? Why are you insisting I go with you?''

Blayne stopped for a red light. "Because I love you.''

"I love you, too, but that doesn't answer my questions.''

He tenderly brushed his lips across her forehead. "You have all the relevant facts, sweetheart. While I figure out who's threatening one of us, you figure out why it's important that you go with me.''

Eight

***

Blayne pulled into the driveway separating the houses they'd lived in as teenagers and switched off the ignition. A huge American flag billowed in the slight summer breeze. Nostalgia, an unfamiliar emotion, made him draw a long, unsteady breath. Closing his eyes he felt as if he could almost step back into the past and see Sunny dashing up the wooden porch steps and pounding on the screen door as she shouted his name.

His hand automatically closed over hers. "Being here makes me feel like I've gone back in time."

"I wonder what it would have been like if we knew then what we know now," Sunny said thoughtfully.

"I don't know, but I don't think I'd change anything. My memories are perfect as they are."

"I might change a few things. For starters, I'd hide my photo albums," she said. "Without them your curiosity to see the four corners of the earth might have been curtailed."

"What started as my playing amateur psychologist to help you through a rough period, to make you remember the good times you and your family had abroad, changed into a spectacular fantasy world for me. I saw myself in those pictures." He brought the back of her hand to his lips. "But I didn't cure you of your aversion to travel."

In an effort to figure out the reason behind his determination to take her with him on his next trip, she asked, "Still playing psychologist?"

"Yeah," he replied honestly.

"What makes you think it'll work this time?"

"It has to work because I need you."

"Self-sufficient Blayne MacCaffrey needs someone?" she said disbelievingly to cover up the uncertainty his admission caused. Blayne had been her Rock of Gibraltar. To have him reveal his vulnerability knocked her perception of him askew. She'd always been the one who needed him. The prospect of switching roles was mind-boggling.

Blayne opened the door. "You aren't the only one running scared."

"Your leg injury?" she asked quietly, sliding across the seat and getting out on his side of the car.

"Right on target, Sunny," he answered.

"You think my going with you will protect you?" Her voice rang with skepticism. "That's absurd. I can't protect you in our own hometown, much less abroad."

His lips curved into a smile. "We'll conquer our common fear together."

"Wouldn't it be easier to burn your passport?"

Motioning to the unfurled flag, he said, "The flag represents freedom. You've let the red and white stripes become the bars of a cage."

"Don't be ridiculous. I'm not a prisoner; I'm free to leave anytime I choose to go."

Blayne stopped on the steps and turned toward her. "Good. We'll forget about our compromise. As soon as I receive my instructions, I'll book reservations for both of us."

"Hold on a minute." Her palm felt sweaty. She withdrew her hand from his. "I didn't agree to go. I said I *could* go if I *wanted* to go. I love living in the United States."

"You also said you loved me," he stated reasonably, then added a dash of humor in hopes of returning the color to her face. "More than home-canned pickled beets."

Her lips pressed together in a straight line as if refusing to return his smile. "I do love you. But . . ."

Randy barged through the front door and wrapped his arms around his aunt's thigh, but his bright eyes were on Blayne. "I thought you'd never get here. Wanna play Kung Fu on my computer? It's a new game I just got. It's even better than Froggie."

With a look that promised Sunny they'd be continuing their conversation, he patted Randy on the head. "Sure. Are you a black belt?"

"Naw. The computer never lets me get beyond the brown-belt level."

"You'll get there eventually. The computer can't think and you can." Blayne opened the screen door and gestured for Sunny and Randy to lead the way. "Does he get you with a kick or a punch?"

"Dropkick," Randy replied. Tugging on his aunt's dress, he whispered, "Mom's in the kitchen crying."

"Crying?"

"Yeah. Dad came over last night, and they went for a long ride. I thought everything was gonna be okay. This morning she was acting kinda weird. But she wouldn't talk to me." His freckled nose wrinkled. "I'm just a kid."

Sunny gave his small shoulders a reassuring hug. "A good kid."

"I guess Dad won't be home for Christmas after all," he mumbled. "Grown-ups don't make much sense."

"You run along with Blayne. I'll talk to your mother." Her blue eyes silently implored Blayne to help distract Randy from his parents' problems.

"C'mon, Randy, let's go Kung Fu the computer," Blayne said enthusiastically. "What kind of joysticks do you have?"

As Randy and Blayne climbed the steps she headed through the arched entry into the kitchen. Starr was standing in front of the sink with a damp paper towel over her eyes.

"I'm not crying," Starr said, knowing her son's concern had been related to his favorite aunt. "I told Randy I had something in my eye."

"Tears," Sunny stated flatly. Her sister considered crying a form of weakness. Setting her own problems aside, Sunny crossed to Starr and put her arms around her. "Crying isn't shameful."

"It upsets the kids." Starr blindly reached behind herself and ripped another paper towel from the holder beside the sink. "I have to be strong for their sakes. I love them too much to let them grow up to be wimps."

"Sit down, Starr. I'll fix us a cup of tea. It'll make you feel better." She coaxed her sister into a kitchen chair. "Tell me what happened." Sunny wanted to ask Starr about the mysterious note, but decided that under the circumstances she had better wait.

"I don't want tea and sympathy," Starr said. "I'm mad. Damned mad."

Sunny opened the cabinet under the sink and extracted a battered copper teakettle. When Starr was out of sorts, the best course of action was sympathetic silence.

"Do you know what that so-and-so said he's going to start doing?" Her mouth twisted as though preparing to say the world's foulest obscenity. "Dating!"

Keeping silent, Sunny filled the kettle and placed it on the electric stove. The fact that Joe was considering dating wasn't surprising to her at all. Many men were remarried within a couple years of their divorce. Realistically, Starr should have known eventually Joe would be attracted to another woman.

"Would you believe he had the unmitigated gall to take me for a long romantic ride through the country-side to tell me before I heard it through the grape-vine? I thought . . ." She sniffed, then wiped her nose. "Well, never mind what I thought. I decided to fix him."

Inwardly Sunny groaned. There was little doubt in her mind that Joe had received a double measure of creative revenge.

Starr began pacing back and forth across the floor, her hands twisting and shredding the paper towel. "We stopped at a filling station for gas. While he was outside the car, I noticed a gift-wrapped box under the blanket he keeps in the back seat. I just knew it was for some woman."

"Oh, no, Starr. Tell me you didn't open it."

"I didn't open it...then. We drove back into town. He knows how pizza makes me feel better when I'm upset." She had the good grace to lower her eyes shamefully, then added, "While he was in the restaurant waiting for the pizza, I unwrapped the gift."

"Well?" Sunny prodded. Starr had stopped pacing and talking. She stared into the backyard. "What was in the package?"

"A snooze-alarm clock radio. I dismantled the cover, removed the working parts and tossed them into the bushes beside the parking lot."

"Why?"

"I figured his girlfriend had Joe to wake her up. She wouldn't need an alarm clock." Her eyes blinked rapidly. "I painstakingly rewrapped the gift so he'd never know I'd seen it. I gloated over what his little cutesy pie would say when she plugged it in and it didn't work."

"Creative revenge," Sunny said, sighing, shaking her head.

"Yeah, but it backfired. The rotten blankity-blank!" Her loving tone contrasted sharply with her words. "He must have known I'd do something outrageous if I found the gift." Tears began streaming down her face. "He gave it to me!"

Momentarily speechless because she had to restrain a burst of unsympathetic chuckles, Sunny turned toward the stove. The kettle whistled as though cued. This wasn't like her. Watching Starr cry usually brought tears to her own eyes. Feeling thoroughly disgusted with herself, Sunny poured the steaming water into the cups she'd prepared.

"He said he'd told me he was going to start dating to wake me up...so I'd see how much I love him...and how much he loved me and the boys. He thought the alarm clock radio might help. Isn't that the sweetest, craziest damned thing you've ever heard?"

"Starr, why isn't he here? You did tell him you loved him, didn't you?"

"I couldn't. How could I explain demolishing the clock? I told him I'd think about a reconciliation. This morning I drove back to the pizza place parking lot. I crawled around on my hands and knees, but I couldn't find all the parts.''

"Buy another clock radio," Sunny suggested, hoping that would solve the problem and she could ask her sister about the note.

"That's what I'm so angry about. I can't replace it." She stomped to the trash can and pulled out the radio. "It must be one of those freebies you get when you pay for a full year's subscription to a magazine."

Sunny shook her head. "Poetic justice. He's receiving over fifty subscriptions to children's magazines for a year, and you got an alarm clock that doesn't work."

"But none of us are getting what we want," Starr wailed. "I can't tell him what I did any more than you can tell Blayne that Randy isn't his child."

"I told Blayne," Sunny replied point-blank.

"You did?" Starr squeaked in disbelief. "You welshed on our compromise?"

"He knew before he arrived." Distracting Starr from her own crisis by telling her what had taken place during the past twenty-four hours seemed the wisest course of action. They'd both been burned by Starr's "brilliant" creative-revenge philosophy.

"How? You told me the letter you sent him and the check had been returned."

"Networking. Men who work overseas keep tabs on what's going on back home. Blayne knew about the Holiday Shoppe and everything."

"Did he ask for the money?"

Sunny placed the cups on the kitchen table and sat down. Her sister joined her. "No. He hardly mentioned it."

"Then why did he come back if he knew there wasn't a child and he doesn't want the money?"

"He wants me to marry him and go with him." Blayne's injury and his vulnerability were too sensitive a topic to discuss with Starr. Knowing Starr, she'd probably say something awful with the best intentions if she noticed Blayne's slight limp. "I'm the one who feels honor bound to return the money in full."

Starr spooned some sugar into her tea. "I'm without a radio and you're without cash," she groaned despondently.

"Tell Joe what you did," Sunny suggested. "He'll probably laugh."

"Humph! That's what you think. When he packed his bags and stormed out of the house two years ago, the last words he screamed were 'grow up.'"

"Do you realize you've never told me what happened between the two of you?" Sunny said, thoughtfully sipping her tea.

"Envy kept me from telling you," Starr admitted. "You were vacationing all over America. I was pregnant with my second child, feeling sorry for myself for being tied down to the house while Joe worked sixty hours a week to support us. Both of you were busy...happy."

"But you wanted two children."

"I wanted to stay home, be a housewife. As far as I was concerned, doing the bookkeeping for the Holiday Shoppe and raising my sons was enough work for me. Joe had other ideas. He thought we'd be better off if I got a job outside the house. Don't misunderstand. I wanted the kids, but my motives were mixed." She took a deep breath. "One night Joe came home with lipstick on the front of his shirt. He denied my accusations a dozen times, but I wouldn't listen. I'd convinced myself I could live without him. Hadn't everyone told me how strong and independent I was for taking care of you and Granddad? Wasn't I the financial wizard who kept the Holiday Shoppe afloat? To sum it up, my mouth overloaded my brain. I kept my mouth shut around you to keep you from knowing what a nincompoop you had for a sister."

"Must be a family trait." Sunny pushed her cup and saucer to the center of the table and leaned forward. "Call Joe."

Starr gathered both empty cups and walked to the sink. Her emotional storm subsided. After she'd splashed cool water on her puffy eyes, she turned toward Sunny. "You haven't told me why you're here this early."

Sunny hesitated a few seconds, then took a deep breath before she said, "On Blayne's breakfast tray there was an anonymous note." She unsnapped her purse and handled Starr the wrinkled paper. "Do you think the sun is rising or setting in that sketch?"

"Could be either," Starr replied after she'd carefully studied it. For the first time she noticed Sunny was wearing the same Betsy Ross outfit she'd worn

Saturday at the shop. "I don't like this. Did anyone know you were there?"

"I didn't advertise it on the radio, but then again, I didn't sneak through the hotel lobby. There were some downtown businessmen I recognized." She was about to ask if they'd been notified of a meeting of local merchants when she noticed how pale her sister's face had become. "You think whoever sent this is after me, don't you?"

"Who would want to hurt you?" Starr muttered. "Like Al said, you could be nominated for sainthood for your generosity. No, Blayne must have been the person who was supposed to receive the note."

"He just arrived in Raleigh. We're the only people who know he's here."

"Let me assure you. Between riding around with Joe last night, destroying my clock radio and kicking myself for being an idiot, I didn't have any inclination to pull a prank on Blayne."

"I told Blayne this reminded me of the police story we watched on television last week. You know, the one where the importer-exporter received illegal shipments he didn't know about. We've got boxes stacked in the storeroom we haven't opened."

"Television is fiction."

"That—" Sunny pointed to the note, her voice raised "—is fact."

"Shush," Blayne said as he walked into the kitchen. "We don't want to upset the boys."

"I'm sorry," Sunny apologized, lowering her voice to a whisper. "We were discussing the note."

"Why don't the three of us go to the shop and empty the crates?" Starr suggested. "Zany as Sunny's idea is, I suppose it's plausible."

"No, you aren't going anywhere. You, dear sister, have a phone call to make." Sunny pointed toward the trash can. "Time is of the essence. Blayne and I can check the crates right after I change clothes."

"The slacks and blouse you left here are hanging in the guest room closet." Starr looked at the trash can. "I can make my call later."

"No time like the present," Sunny said firmly, her meaning clear. Certain Starr would stall if given an opportunity, she looped her arm around Blayne's waist. "While Starr is making her call, we'll discuss our strategy."

"What's going on between you and your sister?" Blayne asked when they'd climbed the steps and entered her old room. Quietly he closed the door.

"Starr pulled a nasty piece of creative revenge on Joe. It backfired. I told her to call him."

"Revenge. There's an old saying about revenge being like poison. It destroys its container long before it damages anything else."

"Amen." She walked to the closet for her change of clothing. "I think Starr has finally learned her lesson."

Blayne glanced around Sunny's old room. "Starr left this place pretty much the same, didn't she?"

"Yeah. She wasn't too pleased when I moved into a condo." Her fingers faltered as she saw Blayne step out of his loafers and lie down on the bed. Hands folded behind his head, he watched her unbutton her blouse. "She, uh, thought I couldn't manage by myself."

"You have," Blayne said. "You've grown up. You're a whole lot of woman, sweetheart."

"You're making me self-conscious."

He moved one hand to his shirt front. A devilish glint lit his eyes. "I'm willing to undress if that will help."

"Don't you dare. The kids are two doors away, and the kitchen is right below this room."

"I'm teasing."

"Oh yeah?" He wasn't the only one who could tease. "Isn't it a male fantasy to have a woman do a slow striptease?"

In Blayne's wildest dreams he'd imagined Sunny playing the role of seductress. "We'll never make it to the shop," he warned with a definite lack of concern.

"Sunday is supposed to be a day of rest."

"Rest isn't exactly what I have in mind."

Sunny gave him a bright smile. "Hold on to that thought," she said huskily as she gathered her clothes and backed through the doorway. His groan of frustration widened her grin.

"Soon," he promised his starving libido, pulling her pillow over his head. His nostrils flared. He inhaled. Her fragrance, lighter than summer wildflowers, intensified his desire to stake a permanent claim on her affections.

An image of Sunny tantalized him. Warm, generous, passionate. Last night had been very different from the night he'd spent in this bed. Youth and in-experience when they'd first made love inhibited her. He'd loved Sunny with the fervor of callow youth; her virginal response had been timid. Only later had they taught each other what felt good, what made their senses reel, what drove them to the ultimate peak.

Recent memories tormented him. She hadn't pre-tended or been coy. Coaxing hadn't been necessary. She had grown into a full-fledged, sensuous woman who knew what she wanted.

Throughout the night she'd responded to his light-est caress. She'd run her hands over him without hes-itation or inhibition. Only total darkness had kept her from discovering his injured leg.

This morning, after the initial shock of seeing his injury had subsided, she'd cried. With utmost tender-ness she'd unselfishly brushed her lips across his scars. That single, magnanimous gesture had sealed his fate. He'd known for certain he couldn't survive without her.

Survival, he mused, directing his thoughts toward their present predicament. He'd considered every an-gle. The plausibility of the note being from someone who had held a grudge for years seemed remote. Like most men, he'd been in a few scrapes during his col-lege years, but none that would have caused a hatred lasting all this time. He'd have to be paranoid to be-lieve the note had been intended for him. Whoever sent the hostile message must have seen Sunny enter the hotel with him. Someone planned on harming her, but whoever it was would have to go through him to get to her.

"Asleep?" Sunny asked, entering the room dressed in a sky-blue silk blouse with matching linen slacks. She automatically shut the door and locked it.

"Thinking," came his muffled reply.

She hung her Betsy Ross costume in the closet, then crossed to the bed and lifted the pillow. "I've decided it would be safer for me to go to the shop alone."

"I'd rather *you* stayed here. I think it would be safer." He got up, extending his hand toward her. "Give me the keys to the shop."

"Can't you get it through your thick head that I'm not the one they're after? You're the person in danger. *You* stay here."

She thought she might have figured out the motivation behind the note. Computer foul-ups could be caused by sabotage. High-tech spying and sabotage were top priority for ruthless, money hungry companies. It made sense for such an unscrupulous company to scare off the troubleshooter who repaired the costly programs they'd intentionally fouled up.

She had to protect Blayne.

He'd forbidden her from calling the local police. But he hadn't mentioned the FBI or the CIA. She'd call the White House if that's what it took. What she had to do first was to convince Blayne to stay with Starr. Then she'd be able to place her calls from the shop.

"You aren't going anywhere without me," he stated resolutely.

"I won't be gone long. You entertain Randy. Keep him away from the kitchen while Starr is calling Joe."

Blayne grabbed her shoulders. His steely fingers dug into the silkiness of her blouse. He fought the urge to shake some sense into her stubborn head. "I'm tempted to tie you to the bed to keep you out of trouble."

"Well," she countered, ignoring his attempt to intimidate her. "I'd bash you over the head with the lamp if I thought it would do any good."

"What am I going to do with you?" He pulled her into his arms. "You aren't going to let me protect you, are you?"

"I don't need protecting. You're the one in danger."

"Sweetheart—"

She put her fingers to his lips to quiet him, realizing she'd risk everything for him. Her lifelong fears were nothing in comparison to the love she felt for the man in her arms. "We've reached the end of our compromise. I don't care where you're sent, I'm never going to let you leave me behind."

Blayne crushed her against his chest. Tears of joy stung his eyelids. The gnawing fear of traveling alone outside the U.S. was displaced by having her close enough to feel her heartbeat. Head reeling, he kissed her passionately.

Sunny felt happier than she ever had before. His kiss exploded within her, lighting brilliant fires.

"I want to love you ... here ... now ... where it all began," Blayne moaned when their lips finally parted.

"The door's locked," she whispered against the side of his neck. Her teeth nibbled his earlobe. Her body ached beneath him. "Turn on the radio."

Nine

"Turn on the radio," Blayne instructed with a smug grin as he backed down the driveway. "Rock and roll played to the beat of rusty bedsprings is my kind of music."

Sunny grinned. "Did you see the look on Starr's face when I told her we were getting married?"

"Stunned, I believe is an accurate description."

"Yep. I loved it when Randy asked his mom if our getting married meant Aunt Sunny wasn't going to be an old *mate* anymore."

Blayne laughed. "Starr isn't going to be alone much longer, either. She was on the phone talking to Joe while you were saying goodbye to Randy."

"So much for creative revenge." She snuggled closer. "Still worried about someone lurking in my shop?"

"I'm feeling ten feet tall...invincible. Pity the poor man who dares to threaten my wife-to-be."

"Careful or I'll start singing, 'Stouthearted Men,'" she warned.

"Betsy Ross sings a patriotic love song? I prefer your version of rock and roll."

"Speaking of Betsy Ross, weren't you surprised when Starr offered to run the shop after the Fourth of July?"

"Another compromise is in the making. Joe wanted her to work outside the house. You're coming with me...."

"And Starr is going to run the shop. Someone up there must be watching over the Peiper sisters."

Nearing the downtown area, Blayne slowed the car. "I suppose it's pointless to ask you to stay in the car while I check out the shop."

"Pointless," she agreed. "I have a new theory. Instead of illicit exporters, I think some corporate spy ring may be warning you."

"Your imagination is working overtime, sweetheart." Step-by-step he'd logically considered the meaning behind the note and come up empty-handed. Instinct alone was what led him to Sunny's shop. "I don't think we'll find contraband in the crates, but we might find some sort of clue."

He pulled next to the curb, within walking distance of the shop. However remote the chances were of

Sunny's theory being correct, he wasn't taking any chances. If someone knew Blayne was in town, he also might know what kind of car he'd rented.

"Stick close," he ordered, glancing from left to right as he stepped from the car. The streets and sidewalks were deserted on Sunday.

Minutes later Sunny unlocked the front door and flicked on the overhead lights. Blayne grabbed her arm; his eyes were on the floor where several envelopes lay.

Sunny shivered. "More threats?"

"One of us has one hell of a lot of enemies." He grimaced, then stooped to pick up the plain white envelopes.

"What does it say?" Sunny asked when he had opened one of them.

"Pay to the order of Holiday Shoppe. Fifty dollars. It's a money order."

"Let me see." Sunny looked for the name of the sender. "Who's it from? Is there a note in the envelope?"

"Nothing."

"Great. The money dragon is back there laughing his buns off. Whose account am I going to credit?"

Blayne handed her the two ten-dollar bills the second envelope contained. "No name here, either."

Completely bewildered and thoroughly exasperated by the accounting problems this money was going to cause, she stomped into the shop. She deposited the two twenties into the band's donation container. "The

Wildcats are going to have their uniforms long before school starts at this rate.''

Another envelope yielded four dollars and no return address.

''Do your customers usually pay you this way?''

''Never. But everybody in Raleigh knows I can't manage money. Do you think this is some sort of weird psychological warfare?''

''Frankly, I don't know what to think. Pranksters don't usually send cash.'' He held up another five-dollar contribution.

''Stick it in the can with the rest of the money.'' She glanced at the money dragon poster behind the cash register. ''Shut up.''

Blayne chuckled over her obvious distress at being burdened with money she couldn't account for. He followed her into the storage room. ''Back to the smugglers theory?''

''I can't think of any way to link the threatening letter with the money, can you?'' She removed a razor-sharp knife from the tool shelf. ''I don't know why you like mysteries. Give me a good love story any day!''

''I'll open the boxes,'' he offered, taking the knife. ''This one is from France.''

''Ahhh, the lead crystal figurines I ordered. They'll shatter. Be careful.'' She hovered over his shoulder, anxious as a kid opening a Christmas present. ''Oh, I love it. Isn't it beautiful?''

Blayne held a small, exquisitely crafted angel ornament in the palm of his hands. He pinched the golden threads attached to the back of the angel and lifted it toward the light. Rainbow colors reflected off the ornament onto Sunny's enchanted face.

"Beautiful," he agreed, openly admiring Sunny. He remembered that rapt expression; he'd seen it once before. "Do you recall the picture in the photo album of you and Starr standing in front of the Eifel Tower?"

Closing her eyes, she remembered not only the picture, but being there. "Hmm. French pastry. Sidewalk cafés. Artists. I loved Paris. It's one of the most wonderful places in the world."

Lost in her memory, she didn't hear the click of the latch on the front door. Blayne did. With one swift motion he set the angel in the carton, picked up the knife and reached for the light switch, plunging the storage room into total darkness.

"Shh. I heard something," he warned, quietly. "Stay here."

"No!" she whispered, eyes widening but unable to see anything. Frantically she grabbed for him, banging her shin against the box.

Her heart skipped a beat, then pounded loudly. Blindly she reached forward, bumping into things as she made her way through the cluttered room. Boxes skittered noisily on the hardwood floor. She didn't care. She wasn't going to let Blayne risk his life protecting her.

"We know you're in there!" a voice boomed from the shop front. "Come on out, slowly, hands raised. Police!"

"Good grief," she heard Blayne mutter, disgusted.

"It's me...Sunny Peiper," she called hoarsely, fear almost choking her.

Blayne switched on the light. Angered by her careless disregard for her safety, he opened his mouth to read her the riot act, but seeing the terror still in her face, he gathered her into his arms.

Tim parted the draperies leading into the back room. "I thought you were a burglar."

"Ditto," Blayne said, holding Sunny protectively and glaring at the uniformed officer.

"Sunny, everything's okay, isn't it?" Tim's harsh tone and the wary glances he shot Blayne silently asked if she were being held against her will.

She nodded, but her eyes remained on Blayne. From the moment they'd received the threatening letter she'd wanted to call the police, but he'd never let her do it. *Please,* she silently begged with her expressive eyes, *let me tell him.* She expected to see a curt shake of his head. She knew Blayne preferred to take charge of a problem rather than delegate responsibility.

"Don't move," Tim warned, misreading Sunny's expression. His hand moved to his holster. "Drop the knife. A back-up car will be here within seconds."

The knife clattered against the floor. "Sunny isn't in danger from me," Blayne said, exasperation evident in his tone.

Sunny stepped between the two hostile men and sheltered Blayne with her body. "Blayne won't hurt me. He's the one who is in danger."

Tim thrust his chin forward pugnaciously. "I'm not surprised. The people around here don't take kindly to seeing a hometown girl being dunned for debts."

"What?"

"Money?" Blayne roared, stupefied by the accusation.

"Al may not be a genius," the officer sneered, "but he's smart enough to put two and two together."

"Back up a minute," Sunny protested, restraining Blayne from wiping the smirk off Tim's face. "I'm the one who's lousy at math. What do you mean by adding two and two together?"

"Simple. This fella arrives in Raleigh, and Starr tells Al you're in danger of losing your shop. Two and Two."

"Equals five in this case," Blayne snapped. "My fiancée doesn't owe me a dime."

"Fiancée? Pull the other leg, buster. Everybody says Sunny is in love with the kid who used to live next door."

"Blayne *is* the kid who used to live next door," Sunny interjected, doing some speedy calculations of her own. She snapped her fingers as she realized what had happened. "Al told everyone I was broke? Good Lord, I've become the local charity case. That explains the twenty-three cents Cindy gave Blayne, the crumpled five-dollar bill and the other contributions shoved under the door."

"Do you or don't you owe this guy money?" Tim demanded.

"She doesn't," Blayne answered firmly.

"Actually, I *do*," Sunny contradicted.

Tim looked at her, waiting for clarification. Not wanting to explain her seven-year-old debt, she took Tim's arm and let him toward the front door. She hoped she appeared to be casually dismissing Al's misinterpretation by asking, "Did one of the people who donated money happen to send a threatening note to Blayne's hotel room?"

The law officer's face turned as red as the beets he'd given Sunny. Noisily he cleared his throat. "I have no official knowledge of such a note. But several people did mention tarring and feathering," he admitted shamefacedly. "I put a halt to that kind of talk."

Breathing a sigh of relief, she patted his forearm, forcing herself to laugh. "I appreciate everyone's concern. Please, pass the word that Blayne isn't a bill collector hounding me."

Tim pointed to the poster. "We thought the money dragon was going to chew you up and spit you right out of business. Guess we got a bit overzealous, huh?"

Sunny cast him a sincere smile. "It's nice to know I have such good friends."

"Hey, MacCaffrey, sorry about the confusion," Tim called loudly to the back of the shop. He tipped his hat, saying, "See you on my regular rounds, Sunny." Then he left the store.

Liberated by the knowledge of where the mysterious money was coming from, as well as the source of the crank note, she made a face at the money dragon and mouthed, "Generosity is rewarded."

What she'd considered to be her worst personality flaw, being a spendthrift, had actually worked to her advantage. It warmed her heart to realize how much love had been showered on her by the townspeople. They truly cared. When they thought she was in financial trouble, they'd pitched in to help her.

While Sunny escorted Tim to the door, Blayne seated himself on a wooden crate and tried to piece together what had happened. He remembered playing with Randy while the postman talked to Sunny and Starr. During that conversation Starr must have said something that caused the postman to believe the Holiday Shoppe was in financial trouble. The mailman made his rounds, telling everyone of Sunny's impending disaster. This resulted in cash mysteriously arriving at the shop.

He understood the reason people sent money and the threatening note. Sunny inspired loyal friendship. Knowing her, she'd probably given away more than she'd sold.

The simple solution Tim had drawn didn't click solidly for Blayne. There was still a missing link. He could feel it in his bones.

Start back at the beginning and work through the clues again, he thought. Something had motivated Starr to give Al the impression Sunny was near bankruptcy. What was it?

His eyes roamed around the storage room. The shop was heavily inventoried for the winter holidays. Was that why Starr gave Al the impression of impending doom? If that were the case, the postman would have heard similar moaning and groaning each season. Al would have been used to it. Besides, the Holiday Shoppe had been in business too many years to be faltering because of too much inventory.

Perplexed, Blayne stared through the transparency of the crystal angel as though it were a crystal ball.

Was there a connection between his arrival and Starr's comments to Al?

He'd teased Sunny about her owing him a child, but that couldn't have had anything to do with financial worries.

His mind came to a screaming halt. If Sunny needed money, he was the logical person for her to ask for help. He'd lent her money many times in the past.

Why hadn't she asked him for a loan?

Had Al been right after all? Were Sunny's financial worries and his arrival connected in some way?

He returned the angel to the packing crate and slowly rose to his feet. Sunny had contradicted him when he'd denied her owing him money, then immediately ushered Tim out of the shop. Perhaps she hadn't wanted to talk about it any further. He shook his head trying to discover exactly what the problem was.

"Sunny," he called in an irritated voice as he stepped through the doorway, "what makes you think you owe me money?"

The euphoria Sunny was feeling burst like a balloon. She nervously ran her hands down the side seams of her slacks, then folded her arms defensively across her chest.

She'd sidetracked Tim, but Blayne hadn't fallen for the red herring she'd tossed out. Her day of reckoning had arrived. Within minutes he was going to know she hadn't grown into a capable business women. She was still the same carefree grasshopper who frittered away her allowance.

Straightening her shoulders, she faced him. "I do owe you money, money I can't repay."

"What's behind this crazy notion of yours that you owe me anything? Money between us has always been like—like toothpicks! Unimportant!"

"Crazy notion? Toothpicks? You always thought I was too immature to handle money." She strode toward the money dragon poster. Her palm slapped against the dragon's rounded belly. "You gave me this monster to be a constant reminder of my inadequacy! Damn it, I'll tell you what caused my 'crazy notion.' You sent me child support. I don't have a child. I owe you."

Blayne thrust his hands in his pocket to keep from grabbing her and giving her a good, sound shaking. "You don't owe me anything. Is that clear?"

"No, it isn't. We aren't kids discussing who owes who how many toothpicks!" His tight-lipped fury fueled her indignation. "If you knew there wasn't a child, why did you send child support?"

He'd asked himself the same question only once, when he'd posted the check without enclosing a letter in the envelope. He didn't want to examine his motives then any more than he wanted to dissect them now.

"Starr said you felt guilty about leaving," she probed. "Is that why you sent it?"

"No. You'd known my plans for months, for years."

The phone rang as Sunny asked, "Why?"

"Get the phone," he said curtly.

Blayne felt as though he'd been granted a temporary reprieve. He had always had difficulty thinking clearly when it came to Sunny Peiper. How could he explain what he didn't fully understand himself? Sending child support for a nonexistent child was absurd. And yet, he'd sent her all the money he'd inherited from his grandparents, every dime he'd had at that time. What could he say to explain his irrational behavior without offending her?

"It's for you."

When he'd checked out of the hotel, he'd left Starr's telephone number with the desk clerk at the hotel, should his employer need to reach him. "MacCaffrey speaking."

Reluctant to eavesdrop on his conversation, Sunny moved a step stool by the wall where the money dragon poster hung. Once and for all, she was going to rid herself of its presence. Whatever Blayne's reason for sending her a check, she refused to let the dragon mock her. Carefully she removed the tacks, rolled the poster up, then put a rubber band around it. She placed it on the counter between them.

Blayne had turned his back to the counter, concentrating intently on the person at the other end of the line.

Ramrod stiff, she thought, wanting to slide her arms around his waist and press her face against his back. His hemming and hawing when she'd asked him why he'd sent the money led her to suspect even he didn't really understand why he'd done it.

That bothered Blayne, she was sure, but not her. She was on intimate terms with impulsive behavior. Whimsicality, capriciousness and crazy ideas were second nature to her, but they were usually lacking in his orderly, methodical mind.

She remembered another time when he'd blown money on her without a thought. They'd been at the North Carolina State Fair. She'd seen a huge stuffed lion she could win at a game of chance. Inside the booth were hundreds of bottles. All she had to do was throw a ring around the neck of a bottle to win a lion. The odds had to be with her, she'd thought. Confident she couldn't miss, she paid the barker and threw the rings. Blayne had chided her, telling her she was throwing her money away. But after she'd handed the man her last dollar and tossed the final ring, Blayne had seen the disappointment on her face. He championed her cause by resolutely tossing rings, spending his own money, until he'd won the lion for her.

She also remembered Blayne's making dire threats if she breathed a word to anyone as to how much he'd spent to acquire the lion. Within hours of returning home, Blayne conveniently forgot he'd won the lion and gave her credit for getting it. Considering that incident, his loss of memory regarding the check he'd sent didn't surprise her.

Regardless of his good intentions, Sunny felt honor bound to repay him. She removed her checkbook from the drawer, hastily wrote out a check and signed it, leaving the date blank. After folding the check several times, she rummaged through the large box that held the peppermints, floral wire and velvet ribbon. She'd put a box of toothpicks somewhere.

Grinning, she saw the corner of the small box underneath a bag of candy. She slipped the check into the box, then placed it beside the rolled poster.

Blayne felt beads of perspiration form on his upper lip as he listened to an associate give him the details of his new assignment. He'd barely heard anything beyond where he'd be sent and his departure date. To say the city was a hot spot of political turmoil would have been a classic understatement. While he half listened, he fought his desire to refuse the new foreign assignment.

Uppermost in his mind was one thought: he'd have to leave; she'd have to stay.

For long moments after he had hung up, he stood statuelike, thinking through what he'd tell Sunny.

Merely mentioning the name of the city would be enough to scare her witless. His stomach knotted with a similar fear. How would he manage to soothe and comfort Sunny when he'd be visibly shaking himself?

For her sake he'd have to discourage her from keeping her promise.

But how? Sunny could be stubborn as a mule once she'd made up her mind. Discouragement wouldn't work. A straightforward approach wouldn't work, either, he decided. She'd balk for certain if he bluntly told her he wouldn't allow her to go.

A tremor ran through him. To protect her, to keep her from feeling guilty about breaking her promise, he had one choice: pick a fight, then leave.

Blayne measured the consequences of such action. He was taking a horrendous risk. She'd forgiven him for leaving once, but twice? If he did manage to return without mishap, he doubted that she'd be waiting with open arms. He couldn't blame her.

Fate had dealt them a losing hand.

"Who was it?" Sunny asked as she watched him return the phone to the cradle and face her. His expression alerted her to his inner turmoil. Lips compressed, jawline rigid, blue eyes shining with concealed purpose; he was upset and she knew whoever he'd been listening to was responsible.

"Business," he replied concisely. "Where were we?" Unable to look her straight in the eye, he glanced at the rolled poster and the box of toothpicks underneath her slender hand.

"I asked you why you'd sent the money."

Because I love you. Because money means nothing compared to that love. Because you mean more to me than anything on earth. Blayne wished he could voice his thoughts, but he couldn't. He had to be deliberately cruel to keep her safe, but the task ahead sickened him.

"Because you're hopeless when it comes to handling money." Her sharp gasp of air, her look of shock made him want to take back every word he'd said, to apologize profusely. But without giving her a moment's respite, he forced himself to go on. "I'd hate the thought of your having to support yourself by walking Hillsborough Street during the wee hours of the morning."

Sunny recoiled as though brutally slapped.

"You knew I'd survive without resorting to..." She paused, unable to finish her retort. Tears of pain pooled on her lower eyelids. Opening the toothpick box, she handed him the check.

Blayne concentrated on the blue slip of paper in her hand. Hating himself for what he had to do, he took it. *Keep her safe. Keep her safe,* he told himself over and over again. Without so much as a single glance at her rounded handwriting, he slowly tore the check to pieces. "Last night covered your debt. Starr isn't the only one who practices creative revenge. I'd say I more than got even, wouldn't you?"

Unable to stomach being cruel to Sunny any longer, he strode to the door. Hearing her footsteps as she rushed after him, he pivoted on one foot. Tears she couldn't control rolled down her cheeks. Blayne felt his heart skip a beat. Above all else, he had to keep her safe, keep her from following him.

"Don't be a fool, little girl. I've always hated it when you insisted on tagging along," he said coldly.

Ten

Sunny recoiled as though she'd been physically slapped. His hateful words completely shattered the illusion that he loved her. Within a matter of minutes Blayne had turned into a total stranger. Gone was her childhood friend, her first and only love. A cold, hard, cynical man replaced him.

Sunny drew on her meager reserve of inner strength and stubborn pride to keep from flinging her arms around his neck and begging him not to leave. Yet, still it was only stubborn pride that kept her from flinging her arms around his neck and begging him not to leave her.

"The phone call..." Her voice trembled, betraying her. "You're leaving the country, aren't you?"

Blayne laughed harshly. He felt hollow, empty. His own laughter sounded brittle to him. "Tomorrow—the Fourth of July."

"I'll take you to the airport." She bit the inside of her lip to keep it from wobbling. The floor seemed to roll beneath her feet. *Don't disgrace yourself by fainting,* she thought. Tiny specks of darkness floated between them. "I won't make a scene this time."

"Don't bother," Blayne refused curtly, denying her access to the name of the city he'd be flying to. His leg throbbed. Shifting his weight, he turned the door-knob. His shoes seemed to weigh a ton as he struggled to cross the threshold. *Oh Lord, give me the fortitude to walk out of here before I weaken!*

Sunny closed the gap between them. She searched his eyes for hidden messages, but could find none. Her hand raised to his smoothly shaven jaw. His skin was cold. It seemed to be drawn taut across his cheek-bones as her fingers lightly brushed over it.

Inwardly Blayne flinched beneath her tender touch. He was doing the right thing, he silently told himself. Years ago she'd loved him enough to set him free to satisfy his wanderlust. He had to be equally strong in his love for her. To knowingly place her in mortal danger would be the ultimate in selfishness.

In slow motion her hand lowered to his chest. She could feel his heart thudding like a bass drum under her hand. A thousand pleas jumbled in her mind, but she said nothing. Afraid she'd humiliate herself, she simply stepped back.

"Goodbye, Blayne," she whispered, her heart in her eyes.

"Bye . . ." *sweetheart.*

Stunned, Sunny watched him until he turned the corner, disappearing from sight. He'd gone as quickly as he'd arrived.

Leaning against the wooden rail surrounding the elevated window display, she reflected on how she'd felt after his previous departure. She'd been ravaged by conflicting emotions. She'd been torn between her desire to go with Blayne and her need to stay safely within the boundaries of Raleigh. Although she'd thought she'd loved him beyond reason, she hadn't been courageous enough to break her self-imposed bonds.

Despite what he'd said, Sunny knew she'd grown during his absence. Silently she denied his "little girl" claim.

He'd spoken to her as though she were a recalcitrant child, but she'd responded like a mature woman.

From deep within, a sense of being at peace with herself mingled with her remorse over losing Blayne. She'd survive. Much as she loved him, she knew she could travel the road of life without him. She'd broken the shackles of her childhood fear.

Fear had once controlled her. For the first time since she'd returned to the United States, she completely understood that. Sunny relished her newfound sense of freedom.

She could have been despondent and bitter to discover that Blayne had returned seeking revenge. She wasn't. Her vulnerable heart had flowered under the illusion of his love. He'd given her sweet, precious memories to help her through the long empty nights ahead.

Restless, she crossed the display room to the storage area. The angel he'd held in his hand lay in the packing material. Gingerly she picked up the golden thread, holding the crystal piece up to the light. The figurine had traveled thousands of miles from France to America. Sunny was consoled knowing the path it had taken was no longer a one-way street.

A flicker of a smile warmed her lips. She wondered where Blayne's job would take him. She wished with all her heart that he would have taken her with him.

"If wishes were horses, beggars would ride," she whispered to the angel, stroking its wings. She shook her head resolutely. "I'm no beggar. I can fly without begging."

The ringing of the phone interrupted her thoughts. Her newfound strength slipped when she caught herself hoping Blayne would be on the other end of the line. On the third ring she picked up the receiver.

"Holiday Shoppe. Sunny Peiper."

"Oh, good. I'm glad you and Blayne are still at the shop." In her typical steamroller fashion, Starr didn't wait for a response. "I've got some good news and some bad news. First, the good news. I've been talking to Joe. We hashed through our problems. He hates being divorced as much as I do! We're going to the first justice of the peace listed in the phone book and retie the knot!'' she bubbled joyously. ''The kids are ecstatic!''

Randy gets his Christmas gift early, Sunny thought, smiling.

''Now for the bad news. We've decided since there aren't going to be fireworks here this year, we're going to take the kids to the beach. That means you're going to be stuck in the shop. Of course, since you'll be getting everything together to leave with Blayne, you could close the shop until I get back and take over.''

''I'm not leaving,'' Sunny said quietly, before her sister could rattle off any more plans. ''He's gone.''

''He can't be,'' Starr wailed. ''The man who called said Blayne's flight to Africa doesn't leave until tomorrow.'' Pausing, she waited for an explanation. ''Sunny?''

''Yeah, I'm here.''

''You shouldn't be at the shop! You should be with him. You're my sister and I love you, but I'm not going to wipe your tears this time if he flies off into the wild blue yonder.''

''Blayne didn't give me a choice. After we found out Al had spread the word about my financial difficulties, which explained the mysterious note and the donations, I gave Blayne a check. He tore it up and left.''

''Did you give him the check before or after he received the phone call?''

"After." Sunny hesitated, recalling exactly what Blayne had said as he tore the check into confetti-sized pieces, then added, "He wasn't very nice about it."

"He wasn't *nice* the last time he left, either. That blasted man is using the same tactic!"

"Please, Starr," Sunny groaned, holding her forehead. "Don't give me any of your crazy logic."

"Haven't you ever heard that at times, cruelty can be a form of kindness? You of all people should know Blayne is a nice guy. He must have a damned good reason for running off and leaving the woman he loves."

As usual, Starr's logic made sense. Blayne was a fine man. Otherwise his savage remarks wouldn't have had such a devastating effect on her. He'd stunned her, purposely hit her below the belt to knock her off balance. Could she have misinterpreted everything?

"He said he came back for revenge," Sunny muttered, sorting through his puzzling behavior, looking for the piece that would explain everything.

"Revenge?" Starr hooted. "Sister dear, take some advice from a former expert on revenge. Blayne used revenge as an excuse. If I were you—"

"You aren't me." Gritting her teeth, Sunny made a snap decision she hoped she wouldn't regret. "I'm closing the shop. You don't have to leave town to see fireworks. Just keep an eye turned toward the airport."

Starr roared with laughter. "Go get 'em!"

"That's precisely what I plan on doing." Her eyes dropped to the money dragon poster. Blayne's generosity would finance her "tagging along." Only this time, she wouldn't be behind him, she'd be beside him. "Give Joe and the kids a hug. I'll write. Oh yes, make sure Al's mother gets the African stamps."

"Good luck!"

"Thanks."

Sunny took one last glance around the shop, then marched to the door. Like it or not, she thought, Blayne MacCaffrey was taking her with him.

Blayne paced the length of the sidewalk outside the Raleigh-Durham airport. He'd checked his bags but hadn't been able to quell his fear of entering the terminal. Palms sweating, he wiped his hands down the sides of his slacks. He knew the odds of any mishap occurring were slim. Thousands of passengers moved safely from one city to another without problems, but logic was useless against irrational fear.

"Coward," he muttered, pulling a handkerchief from his back pocket and mopping his sweat-drenched face. Beneath his lightweight sports jacket, his cotton shirt clung to his damp torso. The midday summer sun shone on the back of his neck, but he felt chilled to the bone. He shoved the damp cloth into his pocket. "It's a good thing Sunny isn't here."

Concentrate on Sunny, he told himself. You did the right thing by making certain she wasn't going with you. She's safe.

A taxi pulling up to the curb drew his attention. Some sixth sense made him move closer and peer through the back window. Before the cabdriver opened the rear door, he knew he wasn't hallucinating—Sunny was here.

His face flushed with anger as she stepped from the cab carrying a small overnight bag. Before he even knew what he was doing, Blayne was striding angrily toward her.

"What are you doing here? Didn't I tell you not to tag along?" he shouted. He turned to the cabbie who was getting suitcases from the trunk. "Take her home."

Sunny smiled brightly at the driver and pointed to the uniformed luggage attendant. "Over there, please."

"You aren't going with me," Blayne roared, taking her arm and escorting her to the back seat of the taxi.

"Right." She peeled his fingers from her upper arm. Determined not to let him dissuade her, she unlatched her purse and retrieved her airline ticket and billfold. "Excuse me, please. I have to pay the driver."

Blayne plucked the ticket from her hand. "You aren't going anywhere."

"Oh? Have you decided to refuse your assignment?" She was ready for any verbal attack he could make. She watched him shake his head. "In that case, I'd appreciate your showing my ticket to the luggage attendant. We don't want to miss our flight."

"Don't be dense. You're staying here in Raleigh."

Faking a sigh of exasperation, Sunny tugged her ticket from his hand and followed the cabdriver as he carried her last piece of luggage. "Careful with that one. It has my wedding dress in it."

"Getting married?" the cabbie inquired, grinning from ear to ear and giving Blayne a knowing look. "My missus and me have been married twenty years come Christmas."

"She isn't getting married to me," Blayne asserted.

Steeled against any attempt Blayne made to divert her from her goal, Sunny merely smiled a secretive smile and overtipped the driver. She headed toward the automatic doors, calling over her shoulder, "Coming?"

Blayne shot through the doors and stood in front of her. "You're being irresponsible. You can't drop everything and leave the country. Who's going to manage the Holiday Shoppe?"

"Starr. She and Joe are getting remarried."

"But ... but ..." Stuttering like a stalled engine, he searched desperately for a logical, sane reason to keep her in Raleigh. "But what about your friends?"

"You've always been my best friend." She glanced upward, looking for the right concourse. "Do you have your boarding pass?"

"Yes." His steps faltered when he realized they were in the air terminal. Strangers were beginning to notice their heated argument. In two quick strides he caught up with Sunny. "It isn't safe where I'm going," he said in a low voice. "I don't want anything to happen to you."

"I'm not afraid, Blayne." She looked directly into his eyes. "And I'm not going to be left behind to live on memories." With that she turned and stepped onto the escalator.

"You don't understand," he muttered. "I can't protect you. I'm having a hard enough time dealing with my own fear."

Sunny noticed his pale face and the sheen of perspiration highlighting his prominent cheeks. A muscle in his jaw twitched with nervous tension. It amazed her to realize he was having a panic attack. She hooked her hand through this arm. "You're doing the right thing by facing your fear. I let mine be the guiding force in my life. I let it come between us. But you're stronger than I was."

"Watch your step," he warned as the escalator reached the second level. "Sweetheart, you've read the newspapers."

His endearment warmed her. She nodded. "I know the risks involved."

"Then for my sake, stay here," he pleaded, feeling like a drowning man clutching at twigs. "I'll be back after Christmas—permanently. You don't want to be away from home then. Wouldn't you rather wait? We'll have a big wedding and invite all your friends."

Butterflies fluttered in her stomach as she neared the departure gate. The flight attendant announced that passengers could begin boarding the plane. Her fingers tightened on the strap of her purse until her knuckles were white.

She could take him up on his generous offer. Since childhood she'd dreamed of a big church wedding with her family and friends surrounding them. What was six months' separation when they'd have a lifetime together, in Raleigh?

Temptation slowed her steps. Her resolve weakened. Blayne was giving her a choice, making it easy for her. From the back of her mind, one word propelled her forward: freedom.

"No. I won't crawl into my cage again. I'm going to board that plane."

Blayne's rock-hard stubbornness matched her gritty determination. He wouldn't allow her to risk her life to be with him. If she wouldn't compromise, he'd have to give. "All right. You win. We'll both stay here."

"No! You'd regret staying now more than ever." She joined the other passengers lined up to board the plane. She couldn't sentence Blayne to a life filled with doubts and fears. They both had to be free.

"You're impossible. Can't you say anything but no?"

Sunny gave him a smile filled with sunshine and hope. Turning, she led the way through the tunnel into the plane. "Soon."

Once they were seated, she noticed he wasn't quite so pale. She pulled her seat belt tight and buckled it. Her skin tingled with excitement. She enjoyed flying, and this particular flight was nonthreatening. They'd land in New York.

"We have a six-hour layover. Maybe I can talk some sense into you by then."

"Don't count on it." She laced her fingers through his. "Face it. I'm going to wrap around you like lights on a Christmas tree."

Closing his eyes, Blayne began mapping a new strategy. He knew he had to stop her, but how? She refused to remain in Raleigh, and she wouldn't allow him to refuse his assignment. Sarcasm, anger didn't seem to work on her this time.

He felt the gentle pressure of her hands when the plane taxied to the runway. "Flying bother you?" he asked.

"I love airplanes." Darn, she hadn't been with him twenty minutes, and she'd broken one of her self-improvement promises. She had to quit saying she "loved" everything from planes to pickled beets. Her breast pushed against him when she leaned closer so he could hear her over the jet's roaring engines. "I mean, I *like* airplanes. I love you. There is a big difference, believe it or not."

"Sweet talk isn't going to get you to Africa. Haven't you forgotten a little item?"

"What?"

"A passport and vaccinations."

"My shots are up-to-date. Starr's a stickler for detail. She kept reminding me to keep my passport current. Next?"

"What do you mean?"

"You're searching that mental computer of yours for an escape clause." She rested her head on his shoulder. "What else have you thought of to stop me from going with you?"

"I'll come up with something," Blayne groused, sniffing the fragrance of her freshly shampooed hair. That, combined with her natural scent, was driving rational thought from his mind. Her forefinger lazily circled his palm. "Stop it," he ordered.

"Stop what?"

He saw the impish light in her eyes. She unlaced their fingers and let her hand rest on his upper thigh. Blayne stifled a low groan. She was using every weapon in her well-stocked feminine arsenal.

"Seducing me won't work."

Sunny smiled. Reluctantly she scooted toward the window. "Tell me why you turned pale as a ghost while we were in the airport."

"I don't want to talk about it."

"I remember saying those same words to you when I first came to Raleigh, but you wouldn't take no for an answer. After I'd told you about my parents' death, I felt better...and I trusted you completely. Trust is the cornerstone of love. Trust me, please."

"There isn't much to tell. One minute I was reaching for my luggage and the next—ka-boom." Inside his head he could still hear the deafening explosion, feel the ground shaking beneath his feet and a peculiar burning sensation above his knee. "If I never saw another airport again, it would be too soon," he admitted. "For days all I could think of was getting home to you. It became a compelling need."

His clipped speech was sharp like the shadowed angles of his face. An errant lock of sun-streaked blond hair fell forward. His eyelids were almost closed. She knew he was scrutinizing her, watching for a trace of her fears to appear.

His glance slid to the slow rise and fall of her breasts. Her cotton summer dress accentuated her small waist and the feminine flair of her hips. He wanted to close his eyes and allow his memory to remind him of how good her skin felt next to his, but he knew that some needs require privacy that an airplane didn't afford.

"Practically from the beginning you told me you were leaving. You pushed me into a compromise. What happened? Why did you change your mind?"

"I thought I'd get a better assignment," he said simply.

Sunny chuckled at a wayward thought. Their destination was known worldwide for its deposits of diamonds and gold. Blayne should be able to get a wedding set at bargain prices.

"Something funny about my job prospects that I haven't thought of?" Given a choice of twenty countries, the one he'd been assigned to would have placed near the bottom. Leave it to Sunny's optimistic outlook to find something humorous.

"Gold bands and diamond engagement rings should be extremely reasonable, hmm?"

Blayne glared at her. "I want you safe. I want to know you'll be there when I get home. That's why I sent the m..." Blayne clamped his lips shut. He'd spoken without thought, said more than he'd intended.

"Money? Sort of a lump sum allotment like the military sends to wives?"

At thirty thousand feet in the air, Blayne's tongue loosened considerably, she mused, heartened by his confession. While he'd been gone, he'd thought of himself as married to her. A triumphant gleam shone in her eyes.

"Yeah. Something like that." The flight attendant wheeled the beverage cart near him. "Do you want a drink?" Blayne asked.

Lifting the back of his hand to her mouth, she brushed her lips against the silky hairs, declining his offer. An alcoholic beverage was the last thing she needed to lift her spirits. Flying high with Blayne was intoxicating enough.

"No, thanks," Blayne replied to the friendly flight attendant. He needed to keep his head clear. Her teasing lips were already playing havoc with his sound judgment.

There would be a six-hour layover between flights, Blayne mused. What a waste of time to spend it convincing Sunny to stay in the States. His libido was thinking of a far more pleasant way to wile away the hours.

"You're doing it again," Blayne chastised as Sunny began to trace the love line on the palm of his hand. "What am I going to do with you?"

"Take me?" she suggested in a sultry, provocative tone. She gave him a seductive wink. "Stop fighting me."

"You're making it damned hard to think rationally," he admitted with a wry smile. He cupped the side of her face with his hand, desperately wanting to kiss her. "Damned hard."

Sexual awareness sizzled between them. A luscious tingle shivered up her spine. The dark centers of his eyes expanded until only a tiny circle of blue ringed the pupil.

A pleasant chime rang.

"We're almost there," Blayne whispered, uncertain whether she could hear him, but not caring.

His lips barely touched hers. The tip of his tongue tasted her, sweet and minty, a taste he longed to explore. But propriety demanded he not act on his desire, so with a low groan of protest he eased back in his chair.

"I love you, Blayne MacCaffrey," Sunny whispered. "I'll never let you leave without me."

The plane tilted as it circled and prepared to land. From the corner of her eye Sunny saw the Statue of Liberty. She pointed downward, her hand squeezing

Blayne's. "Look. Isn't she fantastic? Can we go see her up close?"

Her enthusiasm was infectious, but his plans didn't include riding around New York in a taxi. And yet, how could he refuse her such a small request when he was fully cognizant of her patriotic fervor? Six hours simply wasn't enough time for long, passionate farewells.

Landing gear down, the wheels bumped against the wide strip of concrete pavement. She glanced at Blayne. His face was flushed, not pale. His hand was dry. "Are you nervous?" she asked.

"No, thanks to you," he confided honestly. "Between the two of us, we can slay dragons and face dangerous situations without fear."

"Does that mean what I think it means?"

Blayne tossed his head back and laughed. "Yeah. You win. Wherever we go, it'll be together."

"We're both winners," she corrected planting a swift kiss on his jaw.

"You and me and the Statue of Liberty," he said lightheartedly as he returned her radiant smile. "I know of a five-star hotel with a fantastic view of New York harbor."

Matching his exhilaration, Sunny nodded in complete agreement. Her desire to be with him made her completely forget about her impulse to go sight-seeing. "She's a patient lady. She'll be there when we come home after Christmas."

Throwing all thought of decorum aside, Blayne pulled her against him. "Christmas is the spirit of giving, sharing. You're my Christmas. Wherever we are, regardless of the time of year, it'll be Christmas for us."

And it was.

Epilogue

I'm ho-ho-home!'' Blayne called, grinning at the pint-size Santa Claus beside the Scandinavian coatrack they'd brought back to Raleigh. A recording of "The Twelve Days of Christmas" merrily greeted him. He inhaled the combined fragrance of pine needles, cinnamon and fruitcake baking in the oven. "Sweetheart?"

Usually the wintry wind was still whistling through the open door when Sunny came bounding down the stairs eager to help him remove his coat while she peppered kisses across his chin. A frown etched his forehead as he wondered where she was. He shrugged from his coat, hanging it on the coatrack.

"Guess the honeymoon is over," he mumbled to Santa, who appeared to deny the statement with his perpetual smile.

But Sunny heard him. An elfish grin curved her lips. Not yet, she mused, not till forever. "I'm in here," she called, her voice deliberately sultry.

"Cooking? Don't I smell my favorite fruitcake..." Blayne stopped midsentence, dead in his tracks when he saw Sunny artfully posed on the fake polar-bear-skin rug in front of a blazing fire. She was absolutely, positively, beautifully naked, lying on her tummy, swirling her finger in a cup of fragrant mulled wine. "Well, well, well...what have we here?"

"It's the first day of Christmas," she replied as though that explained everything. Her eyes flashed with amusement. "Did I hear you mutter something about the honeymoon?"

"Honeymoon? I, er..." He patted an oblong envelope in his shirt pocket. "It's supposed to be a surprise, but I think you *out*surprised me."

From the knee down Sunny's slender legs leisurely moved back and forth. Firelight danced across the back of her legs. He caught her seductive wink and echoed it.

He hadn't been accepted in Duke's graduate program because he was the village idiot. With one hand he busily unbuttoned his shirt while with his other hand he unbuckled and unzipped his pants.

"Thank goodness I have a creative, impulsive wife," he said, chuckling, stripping off his shirt, pants and undershorts in one fell swoop. He bound across the back of the sofa, slid off the cushions and landed beside Sunny with a thud. "Hi, wife."

Sunny openly admired his broad shoulders and muscular chest. Since they'd been married six months ago, he'd regained the pounds he'd lost in the hospital while recovering from his leg injury. His skin still had the healthy glow from living under the African sun for five months. Her hand trailed over his hip and thigh as she reached behind him for a mug of wine.

"I've got something special for you," she murmured huskily. "Something you can't get on the other side of the Atlantic. Something . . . made in America, especially for you."

"Hmmm." Blayne sprawled on his side, anticipation clearly discernible on his face. "Mulled wine? That's been around Europe for centuries."

She shook her head, dark curls bobbing an open invitation for Blayne to wind his fingers through them. Her blue eyes twinkled as brightly as the miniature lights on the Christmas tree nearby. "Uh-uh, not the wine."

Blayne took a scalding sip, then set both cups aside. "Can't be you," he teased, joining in her playful mood. "I've inspected every square inch of your luscious skin. 'Made in America' isn't tattooed anywhere. What can it be?"

His hands cupped her breasts, tenderly flicking the rosy tips until they budded under his ministrations. He pretended to glance around the room searching for a new Christmas decoration.

A low groan of delight cooed through Sunny's lips. Six months and she still loved the feel of his hands. She scooted closer, climbing his leg from ankle to knee with her toe.

"It's hard to see from here," he said. "Is that a different angel on top of the tree?"

"No," she whispered. She drew his head closer. Her fingers wove through the thick blond hair at the crown of his head.

"No? Should I stop?" he teased.

"No! No new angel. No, don't stop."

"A note telling me to get out of town before Sunny sets?"

She gave a low, throaty chuckle.

Blayne turned her until her shoulders touched the fake fur. He cuddled against her on his side. Propping his head on his hand, his free hand roamed across the luscious hills and valleys, playfully retreating.

The laughter in his eyes faded, desire flamed, hotter than the fire warming them. Her clever way of seducing him at unsuspecting times and in unexpected locations never failed to excite him.

She called it christening. They'd christened each room before and after the room had been decorated, including the kitchen and dining room. He'd nearly frozen to death when they'd been raking the leaves in their secluded backyard and she'd opened her coat, giggled and flashed him.

His lips curved into the smug smile of a man content with his world.

He knew her secret, just as he'd known she wasn't pregnant when he first returned to Raleigh in July. She'd given him clues. Her waistline was a bit fuller, as were her breasts. Her flat stomach had a lovely curve to it now. Her silky skin was exceptionally sensitive. He'd caught her several times with a secretive Mona Lisa smile hovering on her lips. The final clue had been unmistakable.

"Could it have something to do with the subject of a certain telegram?" he crooned melodiously into her ear. "Could you be pregnant?"

She rolled to her side. "You know, don't you?"

"Ouch!"

"Don't you?"

"Yes, sweetheart, I know. God, I love you."

"Blayne MacCaffrey, can't I keep any secrets from you?" Laughing, she rolled him on his back and straddled him. "So help me, I'm going to burn every mystery book in your collection."

"Wild threats from Raleigh's biggest romance reader." He made a loud tsking noise, arching his hips until he was truly home where he belonged. His hands held her snugly against him. During the past week he'd forsaken the latest mystery thriller in favor of books about pregnancy and child rearing.

"There is something you don't know, smarty pants."

"What's that?"

"We're going to be the proud parents...of twins!"

Blayne chuckled, overjoyed. Sunny never did anything half-measure. She'd always been exceptionally generous.

"I love you, Blayne," she whispered, slowly rotating her hips. She braced her hands on his shoulders, lowering her torso until her breasts brushed against his chest. Her lips covered his.

I love you. I love you. I love you. The words set the pace of their lovemaking. Her fingers dug into his shoulders as he arched his hips, delving deeper, deeper inside of her. She peaked, felt him shudder beneath her and whispered, "Forever and ever?"

Long minutes later, when their hearts no longer pounded and their breathing had returned to normal, Blayne curled her close to his side.

"Forever and ever," he murmured, smiling. "Strange names for our first two kids."

Sunny gave him her brightest smile. "Actually, I thought Patrick and Henry would be nice names."

"You would," Blayne groaned. "What if the twins are girls? Patty and Henrietta?"

"Chris and Liberty," she replied jauntily.

"Aaaaargh!" Blayne covered his chest to protect himself from her nipping fingers. "Okay! Okay! No more creative revenge! Compromise!"

"I like those names." If the truth were known, she'd only just thought of them.

She watched Blayne roll to his feet, grab his shirt and toss it to her.

"Look in the pocket."

"Airline tickets? Blayne, you know I can't travel until . . ."

"You aren't scared, are you?"

"Of course not. I get you in and out of the airport. You get me across the U.S. borders. I'd go anywhere with you, but—"

"Look at the date," he interrupted, easing down beside her, nuzzling her neck. "July tenth. I'll have to get two more tickets, hmmm?"

Sunny stared open mouth at the destinations. "Paris?"

"Good name for a girl," he piped, then chuckled at what was to come.

It was Sunny's turn to groan as she read the next stop on the travel ticket. "Frankfurt?"

"Frank will do nicely. Want to talk about a compromise?"

Blue eyes gleaming with mischief, she declined by shaking her head. "I have a feeling I can convince you to change your mind, without compromising."

"I can be very stubborn . . . hard to convince."

She wrapped her arms around his neck, pulling him down on top of her. "Um-hmm. But I can be very, very generous when the right cause arises. And we both know that generosity is a virtue that should be rewarded."

Blayne held her close to his heart where she belonged. "I'll Be Home for Christmas" played dreamily in the background. "Sweetheart, you can name them Abe and Lincoln, or Betsy and Ross, or Uncle and Sam. The only thing I really care about is our being together."

Sighing contentedly, Sunny kissed him knowing they'd be together . . . forever.

* * * * *

Silhouette Intimate Moments

Available
July 1987

COMMAND PERFORMANCE
by
Nora Roberts

If you fell in love with the fascinating royal family of Cordina in *Affaire Royale*, Silhouette Intimate Moments, #142, you'll love *Command Performance*, #198.

The Prince and the Showgirl: Although His Royal Highness Alexander had requested Eve Hamilton's presence in Cordina, she knew she was no match for the heir apparent—but Alexander was determined to convince Eve that he was her King of Hearts.

Look for *The Playboy Prince*, Silhouette Intimate Moments, #212, coming in October 1987, where Cordina's Prince Bennett finds love in unexpected places.

1198-1R

Take 4 Silhouette Intimate Moments novels
and a surprise gift
FREE

Then preview 4 brand-new Silhouette Intimate Moments novels—delivered to your door as soon as they come off the presses! If you decide to keep them, you pay just $2.49 each*—a 9% saving off the retail price, *with no additional charges for postage and handling!*

Silhouette Intimate Moments novels are not for everyone. They were created to give you a more detailed, more exciting reading experience, filled with romantic fantasy, intense sensuality and stirring passion.

Start with 4 Silhouette Intimate Moments novels and a surprise gift absolutely FREE. They're yours to keep without obligation. You can always return a shipment and cancel at any time.

Simply fill out and return the coupon today!

*$2.50 each plus 49¢ postage and handling per shipment in Canada.

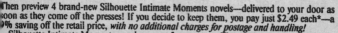

Silhouette Intimate Moments®

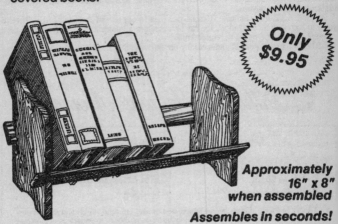

 **Silhouette Desire**

COMING NEXT MONTH

#367 ADAM'S STORY—Annette Broadrick
Adam St. Clair fell in love with Caitlin Moran after she saved his life.
Could he convince her that a future together was in the cards? A sequel to
Annette Broadrick's *Return to Yesterday*, #360.

#368 ANY PIRATE IN A STORM—Suzanne Carey
As the vice-president of her family corporation, Amanda Yates was fair
plunder for Royce Austin. Royce planned on a takeover, and he had more
than business on his mind!

#369 FOREVER MINE—Selwyn Marie Young
Blair Mackenzie took some time off to go camping and escape her
problems. But once she met up with mountain man Dominic Masters,
trouble was never far behind.

#370 PARTNERS FOR LIFE—Helen R. Myers
Kendall and Braden had been the best of friends and a dynamic police
team—until love got in the way. Now, no amount of danger could keep
them from dreams too long denied.

#371 JASON'S TOUCH—Sheryl Flournoy
Jason was a man of many talents, theft not the least of them, according
to Corey. But after one look at Corey, Jason was more than willing to
become a thief of hearts.

#372 ONE TOUGH HOMBRE—Joan Hohl
Though from different worlds, J.B. and Nicole were two of a kind—and it
didn't take long for them to learn that opposites attract.
This novel features characters you've met in Joan Hohl's acclaimed trilogy
for Desire.

AVAILABLE THIS MONTH:

#361 MADE IN AMERICA
Jo Ann Algermissen

#362 SILVER SANDS
Robin Elliott

#363 JUST GOOD FRIENDS
Lucy Gordon

#364 NEVER A STRANGER
Marcine Smith

#365 NO WALLS BETWEEN US
Naomi Horton

#366 MINX
Jennifer Greene

Desire™
PROOF-OF-PURCHASE

FREE!
Never Before Published

Silhouette Desire™
by Stephanie James!

A year ago she left for the city. Now he's come to claim her back. Read about it in SAXON'S LADY, available exclusively through this offer. This book will not be sold through retail stores.

To participate in this exciting offer, collect three proof-of-purchase coupons from the back pages of July and August Desire titles. Mail in the three coupons plus $1.00 for postage and handling ($1.25 in Canada) to reserve your copy of this unique book. This special offer expires October 31, 1987.